HUDSON BAY
EXPRESS

HUDSON BAY EXPRESS

By
ROBERT DAVIS

Illustrated by
Henry C. Pitz

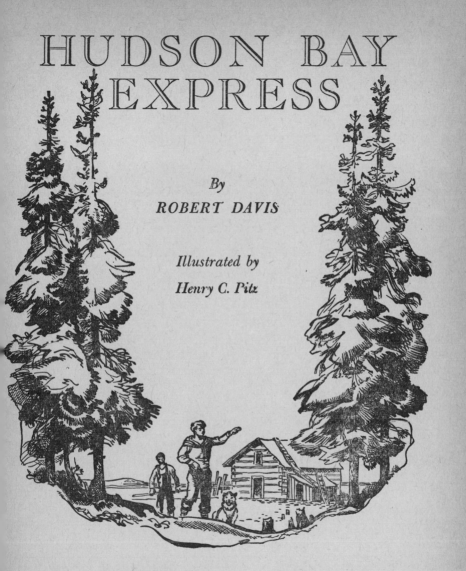

HOLIDAY HOUSE · NEW YORK

1. Sandy Makes a Friend

NOISELESS in their moccasins, and light-footed as foxes, the eight Crees were the first to leap through the door when the teacher's bell sounded for afternoon recess. Out from under a roof they breathed more freely. After them, the smaller fry from the front benches—the whites, the half-breeds, and the Indians — jostled and bustled one another into the autumn sunshine. There would be but few days more when they could play outdoor games, and they lost no time in forming a shrill-voiced circle. Sandy Mackay, oldest of the white boys, seated himself on the doorstep and let his arithmetic fall open at decimals.

Behind Sandy, and last pupil to leave the school-

room, came wooden-faced Little Beaver, chin slightly forward, elbows close to his body. He was the only Yellow Knife in the school. The Crees, squatting on their haunches in a huddle, a hundred feet from the building, scowled as he passed, turned their heads away and spit. They could not show their dislike more eloquently. They were plotting something to the hurt of Little Beaver, there was no doubt of that. The Yellow Knife, obliged to spend his recess alone, descended the knoll upon which the schoolhouse stood, and walked out on the wooden footway, high on stilts, which carried the trail across a meadow of muskeg swamp.

He was called Little Beaver to distinguish him from his father, Big Beaver, chief of the proud but fast-disappearing tribe of the Yellow Knives, and from his

older brother, Middle Beaver. The boy was thick through the shoulder and chest, his legs were disproportionately long. Across the high cheek-bones his face was broad, and his skin the color of weak coffee. His head and neck inclined forward, for a double reason. As a tracker, by training and by habit, his eyes forever scanned the ground for footprints; and as a porter, carrying bales of fur, fish, or provisions, his forehead was thrust against the pack strap that held the load upon his shoulders. The Indian's most noticeable features were his eyes, within their narrow slits. They were not black, as seemed the case at first sight, but a velvet brown, flecked with copper dust.

Within the vacant schoolroom Mam'selle Duval folded her plump hands across her plump stomach and sighed. At this season of the year the young Indians and their quarrels were so terribly tiresome. Once the warm-weather fishing was over, and the nets and traps were being stored for winter, before the brackish waters of Hudson Bay should be sheathed within their seven-month roof of ice, the ancient feud between the Crees and the Yellow Knives, as to which tribe the fishing rights between the Abitibi and the Hottoway rightfully belonged, was annually revived. And so deep-rooted was the bitterness that it even filtered down to the children at their lessons.

"Heaven be thanked," the thoughts of the little teacher rambled on, "that my boys aren't equally divided in number. They can't stage pitched battles, as they do at Moosenay and Deep Pool. Just the same, my Crees hiss and growl at Little Beaver, bloodthirsty enough for the whole Five Nations."

As her glance wandered to the window, Mam'selle was pleased to see the ramrod figure of Corporal Donaldson, speckless in black tunic and blue trousers, swinging across the footbridge. He was on his way to pay his weekly visit of duty and sociability. The little teacher hurriedly examined herself in the mirror that was fixed upon the lower side of her desk cover, blew her nose, and fluffed the yellow hair youthfully about her ears. Bell in hand, she then stepped to the doorway. Recess was over.

While the pupils took their seats, the policeman loitered outside. He was one of the four or five men of the settlement upon whom Mam'selle Duval could always count. The straightness of his backbone marked him as an old-school professional soldier, to the last of his tall inches. Although he lived alone in his log cabin, he shaved every day and groomed each hair of his tooth-brush moustache. He had practiced decency, and loved regularity, all his life. A lonely man, he yet found himself good company.

The front benches of the schoolroom were for the primary grades. The older boys sat at the rear upon planks, behind board tables. As the pupils came from several sections of the territory within which the Corporal was responsible for maintaining order, his weekly call at the school was a simple means of checking up on what might be going amiss. He could learn who was sick or in need of help, who had been injured, who had seen a suspicious stranger, or any stranger for that matter. Any unfamiliar face, in that thinly-peopled district, was the object of Donaldson's curiosity. By reason of his visits to the school every pupil became his scout. Every settler's cabin and Indian lodge, where there were school-age youngsters, was a listening post in his service.

Cap in hand, the policeman stalked into the room, and saluted the teacher, with a smile of mock severity.

"Good afternoon, Miss Duval. Any infraction of good conduct to report today? No monkeyshines or disorder? You have only to say the word, you know, and I'll make all these young rascals toe the line."

The little woman's teeth glistened as she shook her head. The tall officer would never guess what a rock foundation he was to her self-confidence. Without the respect which his visits inspired she could never have disciplined the half-tamed young citizens of the forests and streams.

"Nothing today, thank you, Corporal. Everyone is behaving just as well as he can."

The policeman now wheeled toward the pupils. "Has a boy or girl of the school seen anything queer or unusual? Has anything struck you as odd, or out of place? Either around your home, or coming to, or going from school?"

Curly Bibb waved his hand. "I seen a lynx 'n her two kitten near Egg Rock."

"*Saw*, Curly, *saw* a lynx," corrected Mam'selle patiently.

A bright-eyed girl, in a jacket of quilted flour sacks, raised her arm. "They was a canoe, with a three-corner patch to the front of it, pulled under the bushes where the tree is blowed across. It don't belong around here."

"Thank you, Deb'rah," said Donaldson courteously. "We'll make a note of that stranger canoe."

A little brother and a sister, who trudged in every morning from Broken Bow, were exchanging meaningful glances. It was the sister who spoke. "By the front of the cave where the bear died, they is the track of moccasins toeing-in. Yesterday they was drops of blood on the leaves, but today they is licked off."

"Ah," exclaimed the Corporal, leaning forward, and writing in his book, "That's the kind of news I want. Thank you kindly, Mattie. Don't forget that you and I are after that trapper at White Button, who went looney and set bear-traps on the trails. Any more news today?"

There being none, the policeman smiled behind his moustache again, saluted the teacher, bowed ceremoniously to the school, and clumped to the door.

Thereafter a class in English recited, another in writing went to the blackboard, Sandy did a problem in advanced arithmetic. During the last period, a Cree boy asked to be excused, to help his father haul the poles of a fish trap.

The afternoon session was finally at an end. Little Beaver cleared the doorway in a single bound, and came to earth running smoothly upon the trail that led north to the Indian Village, two miles down the river.

He was expecting trouble on the way home, and wanted to get a good start. One of the Crees was taller than he, but none of them could match the speed of his legs. On the other side of the muskeg swamp, his path left Three-Mile Trail, the main thoroughfare of Porcupine. At the parting of the paths Little Beaver stopped to breathe and listen, and to see whether he could discover any sign of Cree mischief.

On his long journeys afoot he often paused in his tracks, as he was standing now, alert but barely breathing, to get the feel of the woods. One must wait many minutes without stirring, before the timid small voices of nature make themselves audible. He was poised on the edge of the alder marsh. No large trees, save the plantation of white spruce which the path to Indian Village traversed, were anywhere near. The waste of alder had a terrifying allurement for the Yellow Knife boy. At the same time it attracted and repelled. A thousand miles it stretched, to the north and northwest, with never a path nor a home, nor yet a firm spot for the traveller's foot. For the alders sprang from a quicksand of rotting vegetation, only inches above sea-level, and wet as a sponge. With Indian and white man alike, it stirred deep terror. Little Beaver stood tense,

hearkening to the whisper of a trillion branches. Once
away from the path, drowned in that ocean of caress-
ing boughs, he would count for nothing.

He liked to get far from the habitations of men, to
listen to the emptiness. It made him feel the littleness of
men. But to be lost in this maze of elastic wands and

varnished leaves would be more hopeless than to be
adrift upon the farthest ice of the Arctic. This jungle
of red stalks and tapering greenery blinded a man, stole
away his sense of direction. In the end the carmine
shoots, sprouting from the interminable mossy ooze,
would drive him to madness. Trapped within the deso-

lation of the alders, unless rescued through the mercy of the Great Spirit, a man must be marked off as dead.

The Yellow Knives disdained fear. Little Beaver, musing at the edge of the bush, did not like to be afraid. Not of anything, out-of-doors or in-doors. The terrifying million acres of alder swamp were forever there, but a mile and a half from where he stood on Three-Mile Trail was the door of his father's lodge. The trail to it was clear, and he could run like a caribou. With a sudden deep breath, he turned north on the path through the evergreens, and began to run.

At the schoolhouse Sandy waited in his seat until the younger children had disentangled their caps, mufflers, mittens and lunch boxes. He had a message for Mam'-selle Duval from his mother. Both women were of French-Canadian stock, and both from the same parish of Saint Hyacinthe. His errand was to invite the teacher to eat Sunday dinner with her friends at the Moose Factory, or trading post, of the Hudson's Bay Company, where Sandy's father, John Mackay, was manager. After chatting with Mam'selle, Sandy strapped his books together, and mounted the footway on stilts which would lead him to Three-Mile Trail, to the river, and to his home at the Factory.

At the junction of the paths the boy halted. From behind the screen of spruce, through which the trail to Indian Village cut, could be heard the crack of breaking sticks, the grunts that accompany blows given or received, and panting cries of pain and of triumph.

Sandy tossed his books aside, and guided by the sounds of battle, broke into a run. He had not gone twenty feet before he dived headlong. Between two saplings, four inches from the ground, was stretched a strip of moosehide. Sitting up where he had fallen, ruefully fingering his head for bruises, the white boy took in the situation at a glance. He knew, of course, of the quarrel between the tribes over the fishing. The moosehide thong which had tripped him was a part of that feud, and the person who had tied it there had intended to injure an enemy. Sandy suddenly remembered the Cree who had been excused early.

But more important than his own fall, was the fight which was being waged a few yards farther along the trail. Little Beaver, backed against a tree, was defending himself as best he could, using a broken branch as a club. His other forearm hung limp, evidently hurt by his fall. The eight Crees, stones in their fists, were darting in and out, attempting to stun or pound him.

"Hi there, you quit that!" yelled Sandy. "Eight against one is dirty fighting. You let him alone."

Meanwhile Sandy had cut the moosehide from the trees, tied a slipknot in one end, inserted a stone in the loop, and pulled the knot tight. Whirling the missile in lightning circles, he stepped forward.

"Whoever gets hit, it's his own fault. Eight to one is no fair. Get out of here."

As he advanced, foot by foot, the stone whizzed around menacingly. And step by step, the Crees sourly retreated. It was partly their surprise at Sandy's un-looked-for entry into the fight. It was partly their unwillingness to have their skulls cracked. But even more was their fear of what their fathers would do to them, for fighting with the son of the Factor of the Hudson's Bay Company. Without a word, they melted from sight among the greens and browns of the October foliage.

Little Beaver's cuts were not deep, and the blood was already beginning to dry. Gingerly he lifted the sprained wrist and tucked the hand into the waistband of his overalls. The expression of his face did not betray any emotion. Nor had he uttered a word since Sandy's fortunate arrival.

"You'll be right enough now, won't you, Beaver?" inquired the white boy. "Here's the strap that Spotty tripped you with. You may want it as a reminder. I suppose I'd better be getting home. So long."

As Sandy finished, Little Beaver, still without a sound, turned abruptly, and vanished in the direction of Indian Village.

The white boy had almost reached the Factory and his father's warehouse, when he heard the rhythmic pat-pat-pat that meant hurrying moccasins. The Yellow Knife had returned. He had been running fast but was not out of breath.

"You nice fella. Bimeby I do someding you lak." Like a shadow of the thickening twilight, he was gone.

Sandy had spent his thirteen years among the trading posts of the north. He believed that he understood the Indian character, inside and out. Nothing like this, however, had as yet crossed his experience. It is rare for the Indian to show gratitude, still more rare for him to promise a favor in return.

"Maybe he's not the same as the others," Sandy reflected, coming in sight of the kitchen windows and seeing his mother busy inside. His thoughts reverted pleasantly to what she might be cooking for supper.

2. *Old Racer from the Yukon*

IT WAS a Saturday morning, and Sandy had been tinkering around the boat house, when a waterlogged canoe, with only the prow and the gunwale showing above the water line, came drifting down the Abitibi. Intrigued by the idea of treasure trove, and lured by the ambition of being owner as well as captain of a new craft, he had rowed out in his father's flat-bottomed skiff, and towed the derelict to the Company's dock. Upon two barrels he had turned it upside-down to dry, and was taking stock as to how it might be rendered seaworthy, when he suddenly realized that Little Beaver was standing beside him.

In his unobtrusive manner, Little Beaver had become

Sandy's shadow. The Factor's son would come whis-
tling from the kitchen, seeing nobody. Silent as a ghost,
the Indian would rise from where he had been squatting
on his heels, unobserved, beside a tree or woodpile. He
was so noiseless that Sandy hardly knew when he came,
or when he went. He seemed to foresee exactly what
Sandy intended doing next. The white boy would need
a tool, or a piece of material. Presto. Beaver would have
placed it within reach. He might even undertake the
work himself.

Four ribs of the canoe must be replaced. It was
Beaver who brought a fresh-hewn, straight-grained
log of yellow birch, sliced off the slats, whittled them
into the correct form, and with a tourniquet of cord
bent them to the proper curve in which to dry.

The repairs were about completed. Sandy had
daubed shellac around the cracks and was tacking on
patches of canvas. After another coat of the quick-
drying varnish the salvaged wreck would be ready for
a trial voyage.

Suddenly the boy's gaze fastened upon something
beyond the river. "Look, Beaver," he called. "Do you
see what I see?"

The Indian crouched under Sandy's pointing finger,

and grunted. A grey thread of smoke was rising straight into the windless air.

Smoke means a fire. A fire means people. But nobody lived where the fire was. It was neither the place nor the season for hunters or fishermen. The boys knew the whereabouts of all the whites and natives of Porcupine and Indian Village. They were no more than a handful and all accounted for. Sandy continued with his tapping and shellacking, but an imp of curiosity fidgeted within his brain.

"These patches are dry enough," he said, straightening his back. "Let's give the old tub a bath." And after an interval, during which, with copper wire, he spliced a new handle to a paddle, he added, "Let's see what they're doing. It looks as though the fire is at Calico Spring. But no one has used that tumble-down lean-to since last April."

"Sure," agreed Beaver. "Eat there, yes?"

"Good idea. I'll get Mother to fix up some grub." Sandy put away his tools and started for the kitchen.

The resurrected canoe no longer leaked, but it was warped and awkward to steer. Upstream a couple of hundred yards they beached it on some sand. Peering through the brush, they advanced cautiously toward

the spring, guided by the smoke. Most of the leaves had fallen and they could see a good distance ahead.

Framed by the popular branches, the picture that met their eyes made them blink with astonishment.

Half the roof of the lean-to had blown away or fallen in, but beneath the remaining end reclined a man either old or feeble, or both. And certainly he was exhausted by exposure and lack of food. His skin was the tint of a half-breed, and stretched tight as a drumhead over his bones. His frame was big, but muscle and flesh had fallen away, leaving hardly more than the skeleton. Strips of flannel, evidently cut from the blanket spread upon his knees, were wound about his feet. And although it was mid-day and only the end of October, his hands almost touched the smudge of twigs and leaves, so obvious were his sufferings from the cold.

Across the fire from the man sat a dog. The boys were familiar with the breeds of work dog that are the trapland's beasts of burden, the Samoyedes of Siberia, the Huskies of Greenland and Labrador, the Malemutes of Alaska, the mongrel strains of the Indians, and with the color combinations of these breeds and their crosses. They knew dogs as boys further south knew the model of bicycles and motor cars. But such an animal as this they had never seen. Whereas the work breeds all have wolf blood in their distant ancestry, this dog, by the boys' best guess, possessed the blood of the white Arctic wolf, but it had been added no further back than from one of her grandparents.

She was entirely white, and as gaunt as the man. Her winter coat had come in, full, bushy, and spotless, which rounded off the sharpest angles of her boniness. The plume of her tail flowed forward, flat along her back, nearly to the shoulder. Her feet were compact and round, with closely-bunched toes. The breadth of skull between her ears gave space for a brain. Her eyes were deeply inset, within oblique cracks that converged upon her muzzle. Her bone structure was massive, deep in the chest, strong in the foreleg, rectangular in the outline of the body. Ears erect, she watched the strangers' approach, moving to a position between her owner and them, in a gesture that combined dignity with protection.

The man seemed to be in a coma, and did not raise his head. Plainly his first need was food. With half an eye the boys could see that he was starving. Bringing out their lunch, Sandy held a sandwich to the stranger's lips. Weak as he was, the man's teeth tore into the bread and bacon, not waiting to chew between gulps. Sandy knew that people far gone with hunger must be fed often and but little at a time, and gave him no more.

Meantime Beaver had been examining the man's

possessions, which were meagre enough—a rifle, the remnant of a blanket, a frying pan and his knapsack. Rummaging in the knapsack, he held up two cartridges.

"You take the rifle, Beaver," said Sandy. "You are the best hunter. Get a rabbit or a bird, if you can, while I re-make the fire."

As Sandy pawed dry moss together and broke off dead branches, the man was trying to disengage something from inside his shirt. Tied against his ribs was a packet wrapped in oiled skin. His voice was gone, but he motioned for Sandy to open it and read. Inside were newspaper clippings and certificates testifying that Horace Manton had been the winner, on three successive years, of the Nome Gold Cup Race.

Before Sandy had spelled out the sense of the papers and had teased the smudge into a blaze, Little Beaver was back with a snowshoe hare. He skinned it—tossing the head, feet, pelt and insides to the dog—cut it in small pieces, filled the fry-pan with water at the spring, and set the mixture upon the fire. While it was bubbling Sandy fed the man half of a second sandwich. Once the meat was tender and somewhat cooled, Sandy knelt behind Mr. Manton, supporting him in a sitting position, while Little Beaver tilted the pan, letting the liquid trickle between his lips. The man's strength was reviving. He opened his eyes and whispered a few words of thanks. The boys had arrived in the nick of time, at the very moment the Old Racer was fading into unconsciousness.

For a couple of hours they busied themselves around the lean-to. Mrs. Mackay had prepared four sand-wiches for each of them, but they contented themselves with a piece of rabbit and a single sandwich apiece. They gave the dog one sandwich, the bones, and the pan to lick. The rest of the meat and the remaining bread and bacon they rolled in the knapsack, warning the man that he was to save it for supper. They washed the pan at the spring, filled it with fresh water, and left it within reach, in case he should be thirsty. Sandy peeled off the light parka that he wore over his shirt, and worked it down over the shoulders of his patient.

"Are you sure that you don't want to come along with us?" he asked.

The old man shook his head, and pointed at the dog, as if that were answer enough.

"Tomorrow is Sunday," Sandy said. "No school. We'll be back early. Nothing will trouble you tonight with that dog on guard. What do you call her?"

The Old Racer's face lighted with pleasure. "Ne-Nu-Ka," he breathed hoarsely. The boys grinned. They liked the name and repeated it to themselves. A good name for a good dog.

As the day waned, one of the autumn fogs that prevail in the Hudson Bay country was closing in. Near the man's hand, the boys piled such dry wood as they could gather without an axe, threw fresh evergreens upon the roof of the lean-to, and others upon the ground for a bed. For the time being it was all that they could do. The Old Racer raised his hand in salute as they left. The dog stood like a white statue in the mist.

Each day thereafter for a month, one or both of the boys visited Calico Spring. At first the man gained strength and even took short strolls. The improvement, however, was temporary. It might be some illness, or it might be simply the effect of prolonged underfeeding and overexertion, but after a fortnight each visit found him a trifle weaker. He did not complain, nor was he in pain. His memory was a screen, across which marched the events of his tumultuous career. He talked incessantly, sensible talk, thrilling talk, priceless talk about the one thing of importance to him—the training and racing of dogs. He knew that he was soon to embark upon his last journey, and so held back no secret.

And, fact by fact, the fantastic narrative of the Old Racer's wanderings was woven together. Ne-Nu-Ka had had a mate, the lead dog of Manton's winning team in the second and third Nome Races. For his purity of color and his thistledown lightness of foot, he had been known throughout the Yukon as the White Phantom. At the apex of his fame he had returned to the wild. It might have been the wanderlust of the wolf blood. It might have been the attraction of a new mate.

Without his unmatched leader, Manton lost faith in his team. He determined to get him back or to perish in the quest. With a twelve-dog hitch and a full sledge of food, he had plotted a course where the white packs range. Always hopeful, always on the look-out, man and team had gone on and on. Supplies were consumed. The team went lame, sickened, dropped out. At the end, on foot, with his rifle and the white female, Manton battled on alone.

Strange to believe, the lost one had been found. But by the irony of circumstances, when the White Phantom rejoined his master and his abandoned mate, he was in as wretched a condition as they. Manton found him one morning, lying beside Ne-Nu-Ka, licking his wounds. He had evidently been mangled by some younger leader, who had ousted him from the leadership of the pack.

The goal of his search having been attained, the Old Racer now set out for the habitations of men. Meekly the Phantom had followed, taking his third of such game as his owner could bring down. But the love of battle still beat in his pulse. Injured as he was, he had rushed into a band of night skulkers. They were too strong and too many for him. Daybreak found what was left of him stark and cold.

The Racer had the Northlander's wholesome respect for the alder marshes, and although it took him far out of his desired course, he had made the circuit of them. With the last dregs of his strength he had built his fire near the banks of the Abitibi, ignorant of Porcupine's nearness.

But even more fascinating to the boys than the Old Racer's story was the knowledge he poured out to them. He described how to choose dogs for speed and for stamina, how to doctor feet sore from ice, slush, or gravel, how to groom and feed animals during a race, what harness would tire them the least. With minute care he named the qualities of the natural-born lead-dog, the points that would make him the better half of any team. Summoning Ne-Nu-Ka, he would demonstrate upon her body the marks of the prime sledge animal, the ample brain chamber, the muscled haunches that pushed forward the load, the four white stockings that were his own pet superstition.

The man's voice vibrated, his eye brightened, he forgot the hopeless squalor of his position, as he again lived his triumphs. The boys would sit before the lean-to, breathless, hugging their knees, under a magician's spell. They realized that these were lessons from a great master of his art. They must be memorized, each sentence of this concentrated wisdom. For the sled dog is man's best friend in the North Country. He can haul as much as a man can haul, but he can haul it sixty miles a day instead of fifteen. And the man who knows dogs has precious knowledge.

The old man was fondly insistent in explaining the systems for attaching freight dogs to a komatik or sled. The styles of harness, said he, and the names applied to them, differ according to the region, according to the temperament of the driver. When a number of animals, however, are to be tied to a sled for the purpose of pulling it, it is inevitably done in one of three ways: by using the fan hitch, in which each dog has a separate and independent tugline to the sled, and in which, as the name implies, the animals when in motion spread out like the ribs of a fan; or by using the single line or tandem hitch, in which the animals, singly, and on alternate sides, are snapped to the tow or truck line; or by using the swing hitch, in which the animals are paired, side by side, like a team of horses, and the tugline passes between them, like the pole of a wagon.

The fan hitch, said the Old Racer, has three advantages, which is why numbers of Indians and Eskimos employ it. On rough surfaces it permits the dogs to spread out and each can choose his own path. Should an accident occur, such as a snow slide, or an unexpected crack in the ice, with one slash of his knife the driver can cut loose each dog from the sled and from every other dog. Each is given a chance to save himself. This is also an advantage if a caribou or polar bear is sighted, for the dog team can instantly become a hunting pack. In the fan hitch, too, the members of the team are spread out before the driver. He can tell which are soldiering, and ply his whip accordingly. But in this hitch there is a waste of team energy, as the dogs

on the flanks expend much of their power pulling to
the right or to the left, rather than pulling straight
ahead.

The single line hitch is simple, and if dogs are new
to the work or quarrelsome it gives more scope to the
individual, who can, without hitting another dog, pass
from one side of the tugline to the other, and shift the
pressure of the collar on his neck. The tandem hitch is
ideal for narrow trails, along which the single file of
dogs can weave like a snake.

In the hitch by pairs, the couples are called swings,
and the team will be composed of four or more swings,
plus the leader. As the leader is supposed to guide rather
than to haul, he is frequently tied on a free line, well
out in front of the first swing. This free line helps him
to turn a heavy team when they are moving fast, and
if it is long enough he may even turn and bark in the
faces of his team-mates, to bring them to a quicker halt.
The Old Racer himself always used the swing hitch,
which had been invented by one of his friends. Once
the dogs know their work, and are acquainted with
each other, this hitch makes for cooperation and team
spirit.

The dimensions of the komatik and the words of

command, said the Old Racer, vary in different localities, just as do the types of harness. The main consideration is for each driver to work out the system under which his dogs handle best. For his own sledge the Racer preferred a solid framework of oak, 24 inches wide and 10 feet long, with runners shod with iron, and projecting 18 inches beyond the upright rear wall.

The four or five command words used for the team should be distinctive and easily distinguished. They may be in any language, or mere arbitrary sounds. But as each word represents a concrete action on the part of the leader and team, sounds should be chosen which hit the ear with a sharp impact. In his own driving vocabulary, Mr. Manton had borrowed the starting signal of the Siberians, a series of high rolling Rs, "P-r-r-r-r-h. Prrrrh." To halt he employed the French Canadian phrase, "Array," shortened form of *arretez*. For the turn to the right, "Gee," and the turn to the left, "Haw," he used the terms that ox drivers and teamsters have shouted to their plow teams time out of mind. The four sounds differed so radically that there was no danger of the dogs mistaking one for another.

Out of his experience the Old Racer advised the precaution of a stop line, and of a metal bar to serve as a brake. The stop line, a cord or strap fifty feet long, drags behind the sled. Should a driver, running beside his team, sprain an ankle, or, riding on the rear extensions of the runner, slip off, he can grab the stop line as he falls and bring the team to a halt. Mr. Manton had harrowing tales of the fate of drivers who had fallen and were obliged to watch their food, their weapons, and their homeward racing dogs disappear over the horizon. It is always better practice for two men to go with a team, or for two teams to travel in company. Of these and of every matter pertaining to the work dog, did the old expert unburden himself. The boys brought him food for the body, and he repaid them with food for the imagination and the mind.

It was a month since the Racer's appearance, and the winter freeze-up was already due. Bringing the daily basket of food, Sandy and Beaver had hard work paddling against the icy wind that swept down the river. Fifty feet from the lean-to the dog was whining softly to herself. The old man, features composed, did not stir. He had died, then, as he had wished, in the solitude of the bush, with the companionship of his dog. She raised her muzzle in the grief song of the tundra. You-oo-oo-oo. You-oo-oo-ooh.

Evidently he had known that the end was coming, for at his side, held by a stone, was a message for the boys. "I leave you Ne-Nu-Ka. It is a great gift. Save all her puppies. White Phantom is their father. The runt of the litter, keep him too. Do this without fail. The rifle is for Beaver."

He had already told them what to do with his body. Silently they tied against his heart the packet that told of his glories as a racer, wound him in his blanket, and carried the bundle to the stream. The current took it quietly.

They called the dog. She was theirs now, but with her they had accepted the death-bed obligation to rear all the puppies that were soon to be born. Especially the pee-wee of the litter, which dog-breeders usually suppress. That was hard to understand.

At a distance the dog followed. She paused, looking first to the north, then at the boys, as though balancing the two futures. Should her fate be with the free animals of the north, or should it be with man? She refused to enter the canoe, or even to come near it. But when the boys reached the other side she was waiting for them. She had made her choice and had thrown in her lot with man.

3. Under the Black Ice

MOOSE River and the Abitibi unite their waters some ten miles before the combined stream rushes urgently past the hamlet of Porcupine. And five miles north of that village the river ends its existence by emptying itself into Hudson Bay. Throughout its course, however, it is a menace to boatmen. It artfully conceals rocks, its current scrapes together sandbars. At all seasons new eddies revolve. It is a carpet of crinkled, glinting motion, tumbling onward.

Squarely across the mouth of the river lies Crazy Squaw Island, so named because of a legend. A forlorn widow, her wits turned by the loss of her sons and her husband, sought refuge upon these few rocky acres and starved herself to death. In a cave of the island she dragged out her last days, mingling her cries with the hoot of the owl and the scream of the loon. The Indians believe that her troubled soul still moans in that cave, and not one of them would willingly set foot upon the cursed and bewitched spot.

A rumor had reached Sandy's ears that a full-grown black bear had been snuffing along the beach nearest the island. He was fat and drowsy and was certainly scouting for a snug retreat in which to sleep through the winter. His fur would be at its best, worth, perhaps, forty dollars. Even while the boy reflected upon the matter, Bruin might be curled up in some recess of the widow's cave.

Sandy determined to make a painstaking search of the island for the bear's retreat. But he must not rush things. He would give old Black-and-Tan time to get sound asleep. He would give the capricious river plenty of time to freeze solidly. Then he would poke into every corner of the underground room. He was not afraid of Indian hunters getting ahead of him, but some non-superstitious white trapper might. Therefore Sandy kept mum about his plan, not even telling Little Beaver.

There came a morning when things seemed favorable for the excursion. It was a school holiday. The pale yellow sun did not climb high above the horizon, nor did it give warmth, but the sky was clear and the temperature hovered comfortably around zero. Moreover, he would have the good fortune of a free ride to and from the river mouth. Ulysses, handy man of the Factory, was driving the caterpillar tractor to the branch post at Rupert's House with a tow of six sleds of merchandise. Sandy wrapped himself in blankets and, sitting at the half-breed's feet, enjoyed the five-mile trip to the Bay. The ice was glossy and blue-black, and over a foot thick. Nothing to worry about on that score.

He waited until Ulysses was out of sight, then cut himself a tapering poplar shoot ten feet long, with which to feel along out-of-the-way shelves. He had matches and a candle end, but no rifle. This was exploration. Later he would come with his gun for the kill. Yet, search as he would, there was no sign of a hibernating bear. Sandy's disappointment was keen, because already in imagination he had begun to spend that forty dollars. The cave was not large, and he had left not a foot untested. But there might be a lower level; he would try once more. But again the rubble and humus of the stone chamber yielded no trace of bear. Sandy was wandering about, discouraged, unmindful of the passage of time, when the distant exhaust of the caterpillar warned him that he must make haste or walk home. Not seeing him, Ulysses would assume that he had gone back early.

At full speed the boy started to run, gathering momentum as he dodged among the rocks that stood like monuments along the shore of the island. But he had forgotten the dangers of rapid flowing streams, whirling among obstacles, over an uneven bottom. Running at top speed, he rounded a boulder that stood between him and the river. But behind it, kept unfrozen by a whirlpool, was a narrow patch of open water.

He tried to check himself, but was going too fast. He slid along the surface and into the open crack. His body was sucked under the ice by the current. He had barely time to reach up and grasp the edge, preventing his face from being pulled under as well. There he clung, hands gripping the edge of the ice, his face still above the water. He called for Ulysses, but the exhaust of the engine drowned his voice. He felt his toes tapping upward against the under side of the ice. His

fingers were numb, they were letting go. Already there was no sensation in his body.

An indistinct brown face was bending close to his own. A knot tied in a moosehide thong was being forced between his teeth. Instinctively and desperately his jaws clamped upon the leather. "Hold good.

Don't leggo," came dreamily from somewhere near.

A thickset body in faded overalls had the other end of the strap in his mouth and was inching toward the shallows. He stuck the point of his knife into the ice for finger holes, and by this means wormed himself slowly ahead. All the while his teeth gripped the other end of the strap clamped be-tween Sandy's jaws.

It was a matter of minutes—almost of seconds. Little Beaver pulled Sandy into the shallows at

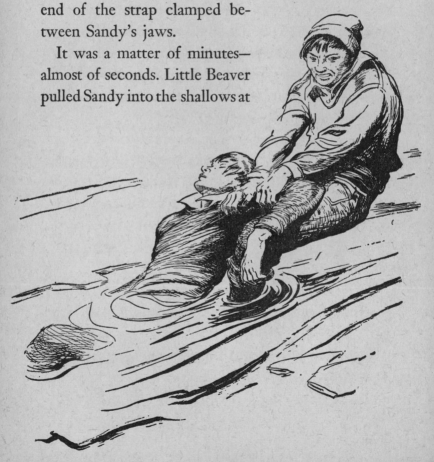

the river mouth, jumped into the stream beside him, braced his feet against the edge of the ice, and in a final effort, hauled Sandy's unresisting body from the clutching fingers of the current. Then as the two boys lay exhausted upon the surface of the ice, Little Beaver threw into the air the far-carrying battle cry of the Yellow Knife Tribe. "Ah-Ah-Ah-Ah, Oyoh-Oyoh-Oyoh. Ah-Ah-Ah-Ah-Oyoh-Oyoh-Oyoh."

Ulysses, urging his caterpillar homeward, sat up straight as the distress cry of his tribe struck his ear. He could not be mistaken. A Yellow Knife was calling. He, too, was a son of that tribe.

The man turned in a wide circle, eye and ear attentive. He saw the long crack in the ice, where the water rushed too fast to freeze. Beaver was rolling someone on the ice, kicking him, lifting him and dropping him, any roughness to shock the victim out of his inertia. Recognizing Sandy, Ulysses opened the engine wide, and made the detour around the open water.

With their knives they cut away Sandy's already frozen clothing. His stockings and moccasins were as rigid as lumber. Ulysses brought the blankets from the driver's seat and the man and the boy carried their cocoon to one of the sledges.

"Take big breath," Beaver ordered. "Sing, sing loud, louder! Roar like mad bear." On the sledge, the Indian was still slapping Sandy's blue face, punching him inside the blankets, anything to get his blood in circulation. The white boy's teeth, all this time, had been clenched upon the knot of moosehide.

Not until they were in the sitting room of the Mackay house, and Sandy's mother and Little Beaver were rubbing his legs with lard, kneading the flesh like bread, pouring bowls of hot tea down his throat, did Sandy speak.

"What was it you put in my mouth, Beaver?"

The Indian withdrew the thong of moose leather, with its knotted ends, from the pocket of his overalls.

"Him, you give me, one day. Him, you say good for keep. You bet, him very good." The Indian patted the lump within his pocket.

Soon Sandy was healthily drowsy. It was beautifully warm and comfy, steaming there on the floor, before the fire. But before his eyes closed, he said, "That strap—that strap kinda holds us together, kinda like partners."

That was how the partnership, which has survived so many ups and downs, had its beginning.

4. Ne-Nu-Ka's Puppies

EIGHT of them, there were, and all beauties. Four were entirely white, like their parents; two had black heads and necks; one was a tortoise-shell, yellow, black and white; the eighth puppy was the runt, the midget of the family. He was coal black save for a white star on the chest and a comic pink nose. The boys remembered what the Old Racer had written about keeping them all, and taking good care of the runt. They called the little one Quicksilver. He was the first to bark. The whole litter would be lying peacefully at breakfast, or lunch. They were busy and would not bother to look up at the footsteps of strangers. That is, all except the runt. He would leave the dinner table, brace himself on his four wobbly legs, and yip-yip his defiance.

On the fifth day, after a deal of low-voiced discussion, the boys performed a ceremony. They christened the pups with a secret mark. "All the dogs we shall ever own must have that mark," they agreed. "We want something that people won't notice, and yet something that we ourselves can discover at once. Dogs have a way of getting lost and stolen, when they become useful. This way there will be no fight over ownership." The private mark was a nick on the inner edge of the left ear. Ne-Nu-Ka bared her teeth when the first pup whimpered, but after that she licked away the tiny drops of blood and all was calm. Within the week the hair had grown and covered the small cuts.

The big problem, however, was food. If they were to be heavy, whipcord creatures like their mother, if some were even to have the speed and stamina of the famous White Phantom, Ne-Nu-Ka must be fed all the seal meat and corn meal mush that she could swallow. But that would be merely for the first seven weeks. Afterward there would be nine mouths, to be filled with bumper rations twice in the day. Adult dogs, even when working severely, are fed but once in 24 hours, but growing pups develop better on a morning and a night feeding.

As it was mid-winter there was no regular supply of fish. But seal could be captured by an experienced hunter. This is where Chief Big Beaver's skill was of immense help. The seal used to be a land animal, he explained, and is still an air-breather. During frozen weather it must keep airholes open with its teeth, even when the ice is thickest. Every thirty minutes the seal pushes his nose into the open air for another breath. Big Beaver would locate the breathing-spots by tracing the tracks of wolves. There he waited with poised harpoon, speared the seal in the head, chopped away the ice, and pulled forth the prize. But it required practice, a lightning quick hand, and a sure eye.

There was also the matter of a house for the dogs. To meet the emergency of the puppies' birth they had driven small logs, sharpened at one end, into the snow, forming a circle, with a gap on the south side for a door. The logs to the north were shorter, thus giving a slant to the roof of evergreen boughs that was thickly piled across the top. This made a good enough makeshift for freezing weather. But when the snow melted the house would tumble in. No, they needed a substantial, year-round house, and they needed fencing to make a runway, and cash to buy two seals a week.

Corporal Donaldson, whom they encountered returning on snowshoes from one of his lonely patrols, had an idea which he promised to follow up that very evening. On his radio he often caught oddments of news which might be turned to account. And, as a matter of fact, it was through this channel that the boys eventually landed their cash-paying work.

"It's this way," related the Corporal, three mornings later. "The Paper Company has bought that valley of young spruce, twenty miles south, on the railway line. They are starting to cut at once. They will pile the pulp wood, in four-foot lengths, alongside the track, and haul it out when the trains get to running again. They want cutters. It's light work, soft wood, and they want logs not over eight inches through at the butt. You don't need to peel it. And you get board and $2.35 a cord, piled where it falls. Looks to me like a job made to order for you boys."

"But who would look after the dogs?" Sandy asked.

Corporal Don considered. "What about Bumbly Bill's Sally?"

At the other end of Three-Mile Trail lived Bumbly

Bill, the one-armed station master, with his wife Celeste and their seven children. Sally, the oldest, was twelve, and literally her father's right hand. But now that train service was over until spring, Sally's duties were lighter. Although a girl, she was capable, self-reliant, and entirely trustworthy. It was a good suggestion, and the boys set out for Bumbly Bill's forthwith.

Sally was delighted at the prospect of ready cash. For fifty cents a day she agreed to walk the three miles to the Factory, feed the dogs, and look after their well being. It was the beginning of a most satisfactory business arrangement.

On their return from the wood cutting, the boys walked with a slight swagger. They had been out in the world, for a trial flight. Each of them had taken five dollars spending money for himself. They paid two dollars for the rent of the cross-cut saw and for files, and they had forty-three dollars salted away in the Company's safe, for wire fencing, hardware and corn meal. Sally had done her work well. The pups were running about, jolly as woolly muffs. And young as they were, they were tramping nests in the snow, in which to fold their tails over their noses and snooze. Although Ne-Nu-Ka had weaned her children and had apparently washed her paws of further responsibility, she was still very much the head of the family, as she was soon to prove.

Bordering the establishment of the Hudson's Bay Company upon the river bank, stood the store of Butcher Smok, formerly a trapper employed by the Company, who had set himself up as a rival fur buyer. He was a blond giant, proud that no razor had ever touched his face, the son of a Norwegian sailor and an Ojibway squaw. On whaling ships and on Grand Banks fishing smacks, in logging camps, in trapland scuffles, he had kicked and gouged his way to leadership.

Combining the forest cunning of his mother with the cold daring of his father, for twenty years Butch had been a better-than-ordinary trapper. But his success as a fighter had turned his head. Being the hero of scores of Indian and Eskimo villages out-balanced his good sense. He conceived the idea that the Company manager, John Mackay, was cheating him on prices.

In Butch's one-track mind, to conceive of a grievance was to act on it, and Porcupine still remembered the morning when, in a store full of customers, his anger had exploded in wild words and flying fists. With outstretched arms he had defied the world. His lion's

mane combed erect by clawing fingers, his nose hammered flat, one ear half bitten off, his beard a tangle of blood and tobacco, a dozen arms had dragged him from the Company store, more dead than alive. But he was a fighter to the end. Regaining consciousness, he had re-entered the store, leaped upon a counter, and in the presence of thirty men, sworn a hair-curling oath to get square with the Company. To make good that oath had been the objective of his life since that day. He had hewn himself a three-room store and dwelling, just south of the Company property. And in the dozen years that had intervened he had never been known to forsake his twin principles—to be a friend to his friends, and to be an enemy of the Company. His great rolling laugh could be heard up and down the river, as he welcomed customers to his landing-stage.

A group of wholesale grocers and clothiers, back in the cities, impressed by his twenty-year record as a successful trapper, as well as by his wife's kinship with influential Ojibway chiefs, furnished him a stock of merchandise on credit. With the rising price of fur, Butch paid off his debts and doubled his stock.

In Pete, Butch had a dog after his own heart. Scarred by battles with every breed of dog or wolf that entered the North Country, the iron-grey mongrel was half boarhound and half mastiff. His temper was such that even Butch judged it better that he be chained during business hours.

But on the last morning of his life, either by ill-will or by mistake, Pete was left untied. Monarch of all he surveyed, he had made the tour of his master's warehouse, and now stood regarding the expanse of river and field, hoping that he might see something with which he could quarrel. He had not long to wait.

Quicksilver, puppy explorer, runt of the litter, had eaten heartily and was keen to learn more of the universe. Disgusted with his stick-in-the-mud brothers, he trotted out in front of the Company's store and barked. He saw the big slate-gray dog and advanced to make friends.

Pete dropped on his haunches, ears alert. The puppy would walk straight into his mouth. Pete's red tongue licked his lips. This was going to be good. For the dog hated the Company and its creatures, as downrightly as did his master.

But in the split second before the great hound seized the puppy, a blur of white raced from behind the Company's store. Straight as a bullet she covered the hundred yards. Pete, hypnotized, watched her shoulder the pup aside, watched her dive at himself. Ne-Nu-Ka knew the hold she was after and did not miss her calculation. She was under the boarhound's body, her teeth fastened upon the shoulder joint of his opposite foreleg. Her head was between Pete's front legs, her eyes and throat pushing against and protected by his throat, her body slinking to the rear, parallel to his own, and nimbly out of reach of the slashing mastiff teeth.

Once Ne-Nu-Ka had settled to her hold, it would hardly be the truth to call it a fight. His attempts to break loose from her grip not succeeding, Pete went stark, staring mad. He rolled, he leaped, he threw himself backward. But always that white body turned as he turned, just out of reach. Always that grip was boring into his shoulder, implacable as a bear trap.

Hearing the rumpus, Sandy and Beaver had run up from their kennel, and stood rooted to the spot. Butch himself came out of his store, and stood on the platform, arms akimbo, a snarl on his lips. He re-entered the building and returned with a rifle.

"Call off y'r sneak-fightin' cur," he shouted to Sandy. "That ain't no fair-fightin' dog. Call her off, 'r I'll shoot the two o' them."

Ne-Nu-Ka was persuaded to let go. Warily she made a circle to the rear, on guard against the man as much as against his dog. Butch walked carelessly over to Pete, who stopped licking his foreleg and raised his head apologetically. The big man rested the muzzle of the rifle between his dog's eyes and fired twice.

"I don't want no dog, n'r no nuthin', belongin' t'me, what ain't a champion. 'N you keep y'r eye peeled f'r the next watch dog I get me. Y' ain't seen nuthin' yet."

The boys were deep in thought as they followed Ne-Nu-Ka and the chastened Quicksilver back to her kennel. Their respect for the dog had gone up a hundred points. Indeed, the Old Racer had given them a monumental legacy. Behind Ne-Nu-Ka's golden eyes lay instincts better than a brain. With Pete's whole body to choose from, she had dived unerringly for the one foolproof spot. She had done it like a professional, with no fumbling, no uncertainty. Surely she had practiced these holds before. Sandy felt a prickle of pride between his shoulder blades.

"Some dog," he murmured.

Beaver grunted approvingly.

5. The Visit of Pere Antoine

SANDY'S father, John Mackay, was entertaining two old friends in the common room of the Company dwelling. It was a homelike room of generous dimensions, the meeting place for community gatherings, such as marriages, christenings, frolics and dances. Like everything under Mackay's care it was a well-conditioned place, the walls of squared logs being rubbed smooth, the chinks caulked with moss and clay, and the whole white-washed. All the windows were small, for warmth, and protected by solid wooden shutters, against which, as upon this night, the winter gales hurled their weight of drifting snow. The ceiling was so low that a man of medium height could extend his arms and touch the timbers overhead. In the center, over the table at which twenty persons could draw in to dinner, hung a double-burner lamp of brass, radiating cheerfulness through a red shade.

At one end of the room, under the clock shelf of fieldstone, crackled the fire. At the opposite end, upon pegs driven into the logs, reposed a half-dozen rifles and shotguns. Bordering the wall were benches, the trunks of trees split in half, and smoothed with a drawknife. Covering the floor were the untanned skins of bear, moose, musk ox, and the wild reindeer, known as caribou. The common room was a companionable place, with a pungent smell of cooking, tobacco, and wood smoke, in which men fatigued from hard travel in the blustering air, could stretch their legs, light their pipes, and exhale sighs of utter content.

Mackay's visitors were men with experience of the north; Donaldson, the regional police officer, and Father Antoine, missionary priest of the Barren Lands, whose parish embraced the habitable shores of Hudson Bay. Among them, these three men had distilled the wisdom of the Hudson Basin.

One of the trio, the priest, had tramped the trails and navigated the waterways with his thoughts fastened upon religion, upon the inner feelings and motives of men and women. The second, the policeman, had dealt with people's obedience to the law, and with the rules of decent behavior, which are older and go deeper than law. The third, the manager of the fur company, had been the employer and storekeeper, whose business it was to see that his men had work and did it reasonably well, that they did not squander their earnings in drink and idleness, that their families did not suffer from cold and sickness. Taking these three men as a unit, all sides of man's emotions and energy were understood, treated with sympathy, interpreted with intelligence.

The quarterly sojourn of the hearty, raw-boned missionary was always welcomed by the tiny colony at Porcupine. Mushing on snowshoes, beside his light sled drawn by three dogs, the gale had literally blown him in from Shiny Dime, that same afternoon. To-morrow he would say Mass in the schoolhouse.

The Pere Antoine's coming was always the signal for the chief jollification of the winter. White families within a radius of two days' travel would make a mighty effort to get to the Post, if no more than to hear the music of their native tongue, and the tales of the genial priest. He was the newspaper of his far-extended parish; he knew the births, the marriages and deaths, who had harpooned a whale or a walrus, what prospectors had struck rich ore, where seal were plentiful, where fishing through the ice was giving returns. Like a pilgrim of old, he lived off the country, the fat and the lean of it. His anecdotes were of men, wrestling bare-handed with a none-too-friendly nature, of those who were winning, and of those who were losing.

He would be in the square room of the Company's house, to baptize the babies who had come into the world since August, to marry brides and bride-grooms. He would tramp to ice-sealed spots where the dead had been laid to rest, to say a prayer and a God-keep-you. On Sunday he would say Mass again in the schoolhouse, and give one of his heart-stirring sermons, flavored with laughter and salted with tears, that were the very voice of the Barrens. There would be a dance, and much good eating, much coming and going, visitors sleeping upon the floor of the common room, thick as tadpoles in a lily-pond.

While the three men talked, Sandy sat in the corner, half listening, his mind like a house with the door open. He was inside alone, but messages sifted vaguely in from without.

The week had been filled with apprehensions for the boy. It had been far and away the most trying week of his life. This would be his last year at the Porcupine school. He was past thirteen and Mam'selle Duval had taught him as far as the sixth grade. There were no higher classes. He had overheard his father and mother discussing what should be his next step. Should he be apprenticed to some trade and become a printer, electrician or metal worker? Should he be sent to some superior school in one of the provincial cities? Should he become indentured with his father's Company, as a junior clerk, and work through the grades of that respectable and responsible concern? It was very disheartening, for every plan took for granted that he should leave his home, his dogs, the open country, the freedom that he loved and wanted to preserve. His head ached from thinking about it. He couldn't seem to think of anything else, nor, what was worse, to find any solution that would let him stay at home. Of course, he must work. He asked nothing better, but work seemed to involve living in a town, inside the walls of a building.

The men were matching anecdotes which illustrate the endurance of the human frame, the hardship which man's body can undergo before it succumbs and yields its vital spark. Theirs were instances of the power of will—especially of a woman's will—to carry its possessor over obstacles. Sandy pricked up his ears, and gave full attention. There was a tear and a thrill in every tale. Nor did the now-interested boy in the shadows miss a single one. More keenly than ever did he realize his blood kinship with the North and its breed of men.

The subject changed, as the men mumbled on, refueling their pipes. How much of the suffering which they had been recounting was preventable? Hardships were due to faulty communication. There, indeed, was the key to a gentler way of life for the Trapland— better communications. Aid was available, if the victim could get to it, or it to him. Isolation alone condemned injured men and ailing women to a slow loss of strength, health, and even of life itself.

The heads of the three men nodded in unison. Better communication was the cure. It would be an affair of airplanes, signals, landing fields, state subventions, telephones and organized canoe patrols. But in the frozen months, with water traffic blocked, it must simmer down to a matter of telephones and dog teams. Powerful teams, trained to cover distance, well-nourished for heavy hauling, strong gear, drivers ready for unexpected missions.

Father Antoine was now thinking aloud. "Yes, a string of freight dogs could make a handsome living along these shores. Many a time I could have used them in my work—yes, and have paid for them, too. But the man who goes into this would expect to do a lot for charity. It could even up, though. He could charge the poor very little, and make the well-to-do pay double. But he would need patience, to carry on for a few years, until his team became known."

Corporal Don knocked out his pipe. "I think he would do better with two teams instead of one. A heavy team, say of Malemute dogs, twelve or sixteen of them, for hauling freight. They would be slower, but a team like that, well-fed, and accustomed to work, could pull a ton of goods. It might even freight out high-bearing gold ore, and bring back supplies. Then a second team, of lighter dogs, for passengers or light loads, like mail or medicine. These could be of Eskimo blood, crossed with some light-running breed, such as deer or boar hounds, or Alsatian shepherds. Every winter I get appeals over the telephone from people who want to get in or get out—they want to reach the bedside of some sick relative, or to get a surgeon in, or to find some scientific party."

The Factor of the Moose River Station had listened closely to the others. He was cautious in his speech, but he was the most practical minded of the three.

"There is also the aspect of dog-raising; that is to say, of perfecting the breeds. You would be surprised at the number of inquiries our Company gets from other parts of Canada and from the States, and even from foreign countries that are ice-bound in winter.

"What I have in mind," continued John Mackay, "is the breeding of pure-bred dogs, big-boned, true-type animals. When we are commissioned by the Company to buy specimens for shipment, what do we do? We pick up the best we can find, without too much trouble. We go to the Indians, but you know the underfed, nondescript animals they have. Their dogs are left to starve and feed upon themselves all summer, and are too weak for hard use, when winter comes. The Eskimos have the best, but when an Eskimo has a top-string dog he will not sell it. I have often wondered why someone right here in our Trapland didn't take up the breeding business. He would need capital, though, and a lot of patience," Mackay finished reflectively.

It was then that Sandy sprang from his bench, and commenced to pace around the table. The idea had leaped, detailed and complete, out of the embers of the fireplace. Here was the solution to the riddle that was tormenting him. Such work was his to do. It was his

birthright. It could belong to none but himself. Since babyhood he had adored dogs, every sort of dog. And at that very moment what incomparable dogs were his!

But he must not make a fool of himself. A prudence

inherited from his Aberdeen-born father sent him back to his seat. It was a temptation to reach out and grasp what seemed a ready-made business. But it would need much more thinking out, before he unfolded it to his father and mother. Just the same, it was comforting to know that the men at the other end of the room were his friends, and that they all three believed in the practical utility of a dog livery for the Trapland.

Sandy kissed his mother goodnight, shook hands soberly with the men, as though this had not been the most exciting evening of his life, and went to his cubbyhole off the kitchen. Lying on his own bed he undertook to arrange his thoughts in some sort of order.

He would need dogs, lots of them, all that he could raise and others beside. But in the spring anyone will give you puppies. He could pick and choose. He knew what ones to take, for hadn't the Old Racer gone over and over the points of the true sledge dog? And hadn't he Ne-Nu-Ka and her pups as models? He would need a big stock of food—but what was to prevent the renting of a seine from the Company, and paying for it by a share of the fish? He would need a partner; it was more than one pair of hands could do. But he had a partner already; a proven friend, who knew dogs and had patience; who was nimble as a cat, tireless as a wolf. Little Beaver never talked, but he knew everything about woods and water and animals.

But what about capital, money to keep them going until they should be established, and trade began to come their way? Money to buy harness, fittings, a real kennel of four or five rooms, and runways for each; a light komatik for passengers, a solid one of oak or ash for freight; even, perhaps, one of the rounded Labrador toboggans that can freight a ton or more.

The question of money was a sticker. He did not want to borrow. Perhaps his father would join them as a third partner. There must be a way, as yet not clearly seen. The wood-cutting experiment had been a money-maker, and fun, too. It gave him confidence. From his father, or his father's friends, or from Little Beaver, an idea would be found. With this thought, he slept.

The first ray of winter daylight found him halfway to Little Beaver's lodge at Indian Village. He could not wait for school to spring his plan. And all that day, going to and coming from school, at noon and at recess, puttering around their dogs, the boys schemed and figured, paper in hand. Some dogs they had, and could have more for the asking. Buildings are made of logs, and thatched roofs of reeds and cattails, all free for the cutting. Dog harness is made of moosehide and moose are shot and their skins tanned by Chief Beaver, who would extend credit. Fish are free for the catching. Two active boys can make five dollars a day and their board, cutting pulpwood. They might have their difficulties. But the big idea had overnight pushed everything else into a very secondary place.

6. *Partners of the Trapland*

IT WAS a hectic season for Sandy and Little Beaver, that first spring and summer. Each of them wished that he had three pairs of hands. So many and so different things must be done, if a dog team were to be earning money when the big freeze-up came. The long twilight, permitting them to work until ten o'clock in the evening, was a big help. But how Sandy ached for sleep. It seemed that his head hardly touched the pillow before the clock sounded five.

First and most pressing was the matter of dog food. The boys rented a fishing seine on shares from the Hudson's Bay Company and fished regularly three days a week, and, when the fish were running strong, every day. By their arrangement, one fish in five was counted out for the Company, but the remainder was cured for winter use. They hired Middle Beaver, four years older than Little Beaver, to help throw and haul the net, to cut the fish in strips and, on alternate days, smoke it over a smudge. They made skeleton frameworks, like wigwams without the covering. Upon these Middle Beaver draped the ribbons of fish and kept the fire smoky with damp moss.

To store the fish they imitated the Indian custom of a platform built in trees. That dogs and wolves should not be able to reach the forbidden supplies, the platform was ten feet from the ground. The cross-bars were firmly lashed to saplings, and it was safe from everything save wolverines and crows.

The boys felt that a team of at least six swings and a leader would be necessary to do the jobs they hoped to secure. They would have bigger teams later, but this would do for a beginning. Using Ne-Nu-Ka as leader, six of her pups could be made to fit into her hitch. That meant the acquisition of six strangers. Later, when they had more to choose from, they would weed out the females.

"By another year we shall have plenty of our own

White Phantom strain," declared Sandy. "But this year, to get started, let's use what we can get. The outside dogs may be second raters, but we'll trade them off as our own come along."

Of the eight dogs bought, six were paid for with fresh fish. One was traded for a jack knife. The eighth was exchanged for a dollar watch which wouldn't work. When a family of puppies saw the light within a radius of twenty miles of Porcupine, the boys visited them. They were prodigal with airy compliments and persuasive words in obtaining the pup whose feet, legs, head, tail, and disposition marked him for future utility when attached to a sledge.

Among the dogs traded for was one truly remarkable specimen, Tleeta, the cannibal. He belonged to a Yellow Knife tribesman, who lived alone, far up the river. The Indian had no information as to the previous history of his angular, tawny beast, but only knew that he was superior to other Indian dogs. His tail trailed out behind, like a hunting dog. He had one white, or watch, eye, which never seemed to close. And undoubtedly he deserved his reputation as a cannibal.

His first appearance in Porcupine had been three years previously. White-Eye was found sitting outside the lodge of the Indian who now called himself his owner. The man had no claim other than that he had allowed the dog to keep on sitting there. Each year, with the first green of springtime, Tleeta took to his heels. And in the autumn, when most of the Indian dogs, who had been left to starve through the summer, were pitiably emaciated, Tleeta would reappear, sleek, pugnacious, and well-nourished. A hunting party had once come upon the dog in midsummer, some sixty miles from his official home. He was carrying something, which, upon nearer inspection, proved to be the hind quarter of a wolf.

"I don't care about that," protested Sandy. "He ate other dogs to keep alive. His owner would have let him die. I like it in him that he is smart and strong and didn't want to die. If we feed him up he'll make a grand sled dog, if he isn't one already. I have a hunch that old Watch-Eye once served time in harness. So now we have leaders for two strings."

Little Beaver was not so sure. "Him fight Ne-Nu-Ka. Need new pen."

"That's so, Beaver. Old Tleeta will have to have a pen by himself until he's fit for decent company."

The Indian was right. With all these animals on their

hands and with more on the way, it would be pandemonium until they built a more convenient dog house. By driving the stakes which composed the walls of Ne-Nu-Ka's first shelter into the damp earth, they had kept it from falling apart, as a sort of maternity ward. But the need of a house of several rooms, where pups could be separated from their elders, and in which the dogs of a single team could be lodged together, was urgent. Until such a center was made it was idle to even think of a freight dog organization.

They were obliged to go into debt for the wire netting, thus breaking their first rule. But while they were in the throes of building it, it seemed poor economy not to construct something big enough and really good. They would not be putting up new quarters every day. This was especially true of the yards. By costly experience Sandy had learned that rival bands of huskies need more than a wire fence between them, if the plague of guerrilla warfare is to be avoided. And he had learned still another trait, dating from the dim past of the wolf-dog. Let a dog, leaping against the netting, get his foot entangled in the wire and hang there, and his fellows, brother and foe alike, will tear him limb from limb.

The house was of logs, and the simplest model they could devise. One end of the logs was set in the ground, open spaces were left for doors, the roof had a single pitch, and was made of poles covered with spruce branches. The partitions, dividing the interior into four rooms, were of upright logs like the walls. Thus it was all logs and evergreen boughs which cost nothing but elbow grease. It was the woven wire fencing, and the amount of it, eight feet high, that was the extravagance, for at no point did any two runways touch.

With odds and ends that were left, the boys also made a lean-to for themselves, with a work bench and a hearth. Here the sleds could be stored, harness hung on pegs, and the hundred and one trifling chores of a dog farm done.

Training the dogs required a part of each day. Sandy blessed the long cool dawns and twilights, when, after a day's work at fishing or carpentering, he would still have an hour to hitch Ne-Nu-Ka, six of her pups, and six of the new dogs, to the light stone boat which he had bolted together for educational purposes. By adding stones it could be made heavier. Never a day went by without the dogs being put through their paces. And no one but Beaver or himself ever addressed a command to them. Those were his two iron-clad rules, copied from the Old Racer.

With each untrained dog he progressed through four steps. First, to get the animal used to the feel of harness, until he was at home in it, and did not try to rub it off. Second, to attach the animal in a fan hitch between two steady, fully-trained dogs, with his collar attached to theirs on either side. Thus restrained, the beginner soon imitated the veterans. Third, to hitch the student in a pair, with an old dog as partner, and behind a pair of reliable dogs. Fourth, to attach a beginner in various positions of a swing hitch, to make him familiar with the idea of *pulling forward*, irrespective of who his companion was, and what his station in the team might be. It was surprising how readily the dogs caught the idea. They hardly needed training. Some seemed to throw themselves forward by instinct, for as a breed, they had an inheritance of centuries of service as draught animals. Occasionally a raw dog would be terrified by the bind of the harness. After one or two slight bites from frightened youngsters, Sandy got into the habit of wearing leather mitts for training.

For the words of command used in driving their dogs, Sandy and Beaver used the phrases which the

Old Racer had found good. To them they added the term of encouragement that is universal in dogdom: Mush, Get along, derived from *Marchez, Marche*.

Summer's finale came at last, and the partners took stock of where they stood. For six weeks they had taken turns, week in and week out. One always remained at home for the daily lesson, the other cut pulp wood, to bring in cash money. They had also worked as laborers for the Company, unloading the flatboats that brought the annual stock of supplies by water. Now the snow had come and they were prepared to accept business, if it should turn up. The "if" was sickeningly big, for they owed what seemed an enormous sum. The inventory of their business as Sandy wrote it out on the common room table was as follows:

We own

1	*Overhead Platform, and Stock of Smoked Fish*	$80.00
1	*Kennel, with Runways*	60.00
1	*Dog Harness, Padded Collars, Snaps*	10.00
1	*Second-Hand Komatik, Repaired*	7.00
1	*Team, Thirteen Dogs*	100.00
14	*Assorted Puppies*	50.00
2	*Adult Dogs*	20.00
	Total	$327.00

We owe

For Nails, Fence, Harness Rings and Snaps	$47.00
For Tanning 3 Moose Hides, Chief Beaver	9.00
For 8 Days' Work, Middle Beaver	12.00
For 20 Days' Kennel Care, Sally	10.00
Total	$78.00

Sandy scowled at the figures. "Gee, but I hate to owe anything to anybody."

Beaver looked up from the paddle blade he was scraping. "Maybe we get job, yes?"

It was that same night that Corporal Donaldson, meeting them as they went to the fortnightly train, remarked, "Is that team of yours fit for work?"

"Indeed they are," replied Sandy heartily. "I've had them out every day. Their feet are hard. They cover snow like old-timers. Why?"

"I may have your first customer for you. We'll see who comes on the train tonight."

7. A Stranger in the Night

SUMMER comes to an official close at Porcupine with the arrival of the last train. Although the regular open-season schedule is not overcrowded, there being but one train a fortnight, the arrival of that fortnightly wood-burner always left a future, since there was still another one to look forward to. But the Last Train of the Year was different. It locked a door. After that, for seven months, little Porcupine would be a prisoner of the cold. The Last Train ushered in the monotonous, inhuman silence, the ice blockade, the twenty-foot snow-falls. The boys never let anything prevent their being on hand when Old Cannonball pulled alongside the dismantled freight car which served as passenger depot and as Bumbly Bill's office. But tonight they were there for a special reason.

It was three o'clock in the morning. A hundred silent figures muffled within folds of wool and fur, had been waiting for two hours in the flaky snow, when the bright eye of the headlight crept into sight. Sandy often wondered where so numerous a crowd could come from. Did they burrow out of the snow like fur-bearing animals? Swarthed within parkas, with only Bumbly Bill's two lanterns to dispel the darkness, few could be recognized. Hardly a voice spoke. They were there because they were lonesome and curious to stare at new arrivals, to envy those who received express packages, to pick up such bits of gossip as they might chance to overhear.

The Last Train, amid dead silence, slowed to a stop. Like the red bow of a wooden ship, the shield of the snowplow came first, propelled by its own locomotive. Coupled to this engine was the regular-duty locomotive, a passenger car and a baggage car. To the patient waiters, that second car was bringing the last reading matter, the last clothing, the last medicine, the last fruit and fresh food, until the chinook wind should melt the drifts to rivulets.

Behind the shield of the plow perched six men, the shovellers. They were young men, picked for muscle and endurance. Their task, when the engine wheels, grinding slower and slower, panted to a hissing stand-still, unable to nose aside the weight, was to scramble out ahead and dig away the white hillock for a fresh start. They wore mukluks tied above the knee, the moccasin feet of which were of moosehide, and the leg of the uncut, whole skin of a seal.

The passenger car was jammed, for this was the last day allowed by law for turning in the pelts of the beaver season. Following the date when the hunting of these fur-bearers becomes unlawful—that they may rear their new families undisturbed—twenty days are allowed the trapper to dry his skins, sell them, or trade them at the store. Every man in the passenger car had a pack, tightly encased in caribou hide, or canvas. It might be large or it might be small, depending upon his luck and skill. An electric undercurrent of talk was in the air. People were whispering that a prime beaver pelt would bring sixty dollars, an unheard-of price. At the farther end of Three-Mile Trail the lamps would be blazing all night in the stores of the Bay Company, and the rival, Butch Smok. There would be little sleep in Porcupine that night, for Indian, white man, or half-breed.

The train crew and the shovellers had been on the road since daybreak of the previous day. But more nerve-racking to the crew than bucking snow, was the nonchalant habit of their prospective passengers to camp on the track. The engineer had been unable to run faster than fifteen miles an hour for fear of committing murder.

The man of the wilderness is governed by the seasons, the weather, the sun and the moon. This man has no machines. He has neither clock nor calendar. The train is scheduled to pass a given tree every fourteen sunrises. But he loses count of the sunrises, for each is similar to the one that went before. And as to the hour of day that the train will appear, even the conductor cannot foretell that.

Wherefore the trapper, whose business requires a trainride, makes a guess. He brings his dogs, his wife, his children and his grandparents to the railway line, makes camp in the middle of the track and waits. He is confident that the train will not sneak by unnoticed. His dogs keep guard during the day and at night he feeds a bright campfire. When the engineer hears barking dogs or sees a fire he jams on the brakes, with a prayer that it may not be too late. It is all very first-cousin-like. The engineer shouts his greetings, the would-be passengers grab the papooses and the soup kettle by the nearest handle, and climb aboard. Even the fireman jumps down to lend grandmother a shoulder, for that lower step of the car is terribly high, and she is dumpy.

Ruddy Brick, the brakeman, unlatched the door of the passenger car and let the gale hurl it open. He was a man of a single joke, but loved that joke dearly. Knowing that this was his last chance for six months to use it, he whacked his mittened hands together and cleared his throat.

"Ladies and gents, this here is Porcupine, our last stop. Next station, the North Pole. But you gotta swim, skate, fly, or go afoot from here, and carry your own baggage."

As usual, no laughter greeted the familiar joke. From the crowded passenger car, heavy with the fumes of greasy leather and unwashed bodies, came only the soft scrape of moccasins, grunts, and sibilant whisperings. Sleeping trappers awoke, gathered their thick-set wives and children, their bales of bedding, and their packs of beaver pelts, and stiffly descended to the waiting crowd. Apparently, not a word of greeting was spoken by any one.

The white man, his sense of hearing dulled by the noise of towns, does not at first understand how wilderness people communicate among themselves. Many of their words are too low for the white man's ear to catch. Members of a family, or near friends, may meet after a separation of six months or a year. They do not burst into laughter or loud talk. They hardly seem to recognize one another. There is a slight movement of eyebrows and shoulders, a grunt, a nod, and a wave of the hand. But each has told his story. They have imparted the news, the name of the new baby, the size and quality of the fur catch, and the price they expect to get.

None the less, it is a gala event, this last trading trip of the year. Prime beaver pelts will bring top prices. There will be plenty of credit for everything. The united family will stand at the storekeeper's elbow when he measures out the bacon, flour, beans, tea, and sugar, red-brown eyes not missing a single motion. The men will need new traps, ammunition, an axe head, perhaps a bit of tobacco. The wives have come to make

sure that plenty of blanketing, needles and strong thread, yarn, calico, and gaudy ribbons are included in the barter. The boys and girls want new records for their phonograph with the big blue horn.

Soon the last papoose and dog have been swallowed into the storm headed for the trading posts. The crowd that awaited the Last Train has vanished as silently and mysteriously as it assembled.

Sandy and Beaver found themselves alone. Corporal Don had been there, towering above the others. He had scanned the face of each arrival, but evidently his man was not among them, for he had gone home alone.

Sally was closing up the freight-car office, managing

her father in the high-handed manner she assumed before company. She put the money drawer and the bundle of tickets into the safe, took the key from Bill's pocket, locked the safe, and put the key back in his pocket. Climbing upon a box, she blew out the lantern. She pushed her father outdoors, snapped the padlock which secured the door, and arm-in-arm, father and daughter took the trail to the cabin, where Celeste and the six younger children were asleep.

The boys fell into step behind Bill and Sally. But Sandy felt a sort of sickness all over. A heavy feeling inside, like a stone. He had worked so hard all summer, to get the team in working shape. It was a young team, to be sure, not yet fit for any knock-down-and-drag-out expedition. The komatik was second hand, but it had new thongs at every joint. The dogs were chock-full of good-will, and Ne-Nu-Ka handled them like a machine. The boy stopped on the footway, rubbing his fingers into his tired eyes. He was disappointed, disgusted with dogs and people.

"I guess I counted too much on that passenger of the Corporal's who didn't come," he said to Beaver. "That's my trouble. I see a little and I jump at the rest. And mostly I guess wrong. But I sure did count on a trip for that man. And there wasn't even a message." Without a further word between them, Sandy knew that his partner was plunged in the same gloom as himself.

That same night, however, none of those who waited at the Porcupine depot had been so situated as to catch a glimpse of the nervous figure who dropped from the off-side of the baggage car before the train had come to a halt. In one hand he held a valise. Over his shoulder, supported by a strap, was a metal case, of much the same dimensions as an orange crate. Under the weight of the case the man floundered in the snow, making no progress. He then unloosed one end of the shoulder strap and hauled the box, sled-wise, into the shadow of a coal pocket. Seating himself upon his baggage, the stranger composed himself to wait.

The Last Train was about ready for bed. The brakeman blew out the kerosene lamps and banked the fire in the passenger car. The engine crews and shovellers ran their machines upon the turntable, and creakingly swung them to face southward. The clinkers were cleaned from the fireboxes. All was ready for the return voyage which was to begin at daylight. With grunts and sighs of weariness the trainmen unrolled their mattresses upon the baggage-car floor, drank deep from the bucket of tea which the baggage-man had brewed, and swam effortlessly out upon an ocean of snores and slumber.

The watcher by the coal pocket had as yet made no movement. Across the six miles of frozen muskeg and alder swamp, he could hear the grating and rasping of the cakes of shore ice breaking against one another on the edge of the Bay. It had now stopped snowing. Triangles of green and orange, pale polar colorings, shot into the sky for an instant. The watcher waited until the visible landscape, in all of its parts, had been without sound or movement for fifteen minutes, then he rose. He lifted his box judiciously, and decided against trying to pack so heavy a burden. Valise in hand, he left the shelter of the sleeping train and walked quickly eastward upon Three-Mile Trail. At the policeman's door he knocked, and spoke low to the person inside, who, still dressed, was waiting up for him.

"Is your traineau handy, Corporal?" inquired the stranger. "The equipment weighs even more than I thought." The policeman stepped to his firewood shed, reached a handsled down from its peg, and entered his cabin for outdoor clothing.

"No, not you, Don," objected the new-comer. "I'll bring it alone. You keep the radio connection. Stutter around, trying for secondary contacts. Write down cipher messages. It'll save time when my apparatus gets to functioning." Turning on his heel, the stranger was gone.

★ ★ ★

Two heavy-eyed men lifted off their head-sets and began to unlace their shoes. It was after six o'clock in the morning.

"It's that hut on Sable Island right enough," said the stranger. "If the boy can be ready I'll push off tonight. Just the two of us, young Mackay and myself."

8. The Hut on Sable Island

IN THE starchy tone that he reserved for police matters, the Corporal was concluding his remarks. It was before breakfast on the morning following the arrival of the Last Train, and he had beckoned Sandy away from his chores in the dog-yard.

"To make sure you understand, I will repeat the Lieutenant's instructions. You and your team are to be on the ice, a hundred yards below the Company's warehouse, at twelve o'clock tonight. Do not speak of this trip, except to your father and to Beaver. Take five days' rations for the Lieutenant, yourself and the dogs. You will travel only by night. The distances are short. The dogs must be close-tied during the day, so take chains. You cannot make a fire, so pack a spirit lamp. The wages are twenty-five dollars a day, part days to count as whole days, payable in cash on your return. The Lieutenant's trunk will weigh about one hundred and fifty pounds. You are under his orders. Is everything clear?"

Sandy's manner was matter-of-fact but his thoughts were turning summersaults. Now that his big opportunity had come he was scared; he was half-tempted to wriggle out of it. This was the first time that his green team and he, its amateur driver, had hired out to strangers. He was only fourteen. The secrecy upon which Donaldson insisted showed that the business was risky. On the other hand, he would be under the orders of a seasoned, older man. His job was simple, to feed his dogs and make them run where and when he was commanded. Nothing more than that. As to his team, for short hauls, he would bet dollars against a pickled fish on its courage and obedience.

The Corporal unbent sufficiently to offer last-minute encouragement. "This first trip is in the nature of a scouting party. The Lieutenant wants to get the lay of the land. If you satisfy him, there may be a bigger trip."

With fresh thanks to the policeman, Sandy galloped

off to break the news to his father and partner. The Corporal had come through with a first customer.

The boys packed the dog ration for each day separately, in a burlap sack. It would be less cumbersome that way, and Sandy would not make the mistake of overfeeding, and being caught short on the last meal. They took the team for a ten-mile dress rehearsal. Offshore, fog shrouded the Bay. On the river the surface of the ice was better-than-fair, with few fissures and little drifted snow. For quarter-mile stretches the wind had swept it as bare as window panes. Sandy did not know the Lieutenant's destination, but he was relieved that the weather signs did not indicate storm or high wind. The temperature was ten below zero; nice, middling weather for a trip. The boys tried to imagine every item that could possibly be needed: sleeping bags, food in cans, alcohol for cooking, matches, flashlight, iron stakes for the dogs' tether line, the fifty-foot stop line.

Looking ahead to the training of a second team, they had already bolted runners under the stone-boat. Upon ice or hard crust, it served tolerably well. During Sandy's absence, Beaver was to devote his whole time to shaping Tleeta as a leader, and five or six young dogs who were strong enough to work. Though no more than half-trained, a small second string might have its use in the near future. They could trail along behind their kennel-mates, at any rate, and Beaver's magnificent legs would let him run beside the lead-dog, which would go far to compensate for their lack of experience.

It was one minute to midnight, when a single figure, hauling a handsled, approached Sandy at the rendez-vous. It was Corporal Don.

"Not wanting to be seen," he explained, "I came round by the middle trail. The Lieutenant will be along directly. I do not think that anyone suspects that he is in Porcupine. You are lucky to be under such a man. Study him. Copy him."

As they shifted the metal box from the handsled to the komatik, making it secure with cord, a third shape floated out from the river bank like a puff of mist. He was camouflaged to perfection. His moccasins made no sound. His parka, mittens and lower clothing were white. He shook hands with Sandy, offered a low-voiced compliment upon the appearance of the dogs, found a seat among the duffle bags, returned Donaldson's military salute, and said, "Let's go, Driver."

Sandy spoke to Ne-Nu-Ka, not daring to whistle. She understood. During the trip he would trot alongside his team or stand upon the ends of the runners. Under his hand, convenient to steady himself, were the back uprights of the sled's frame.

"Take the middle of the stream, and go five miles out upon the Bay," the Lieutenant ordered crisply. "I'll give you the course then."

Ne-Nu-Ka set a fast trot, which she quickened to an easy lope. As they swung past the ledge upon which Indian Village slept, the friction of claws upon ice barely audible, a village dog lifted his mournful voice. Sandy turned, smiling. His partner had seen him pass, on the first trip of the Hudson Bay Express.

Five miles from shore, Sandy called "Array" to Ne-Nu-Ka, and turned to the officer for orders.

"Our objective," said the Lieutenant, "is the small harbor at the northeast corner of Sable Island. The hut that is to be investigated is on the southwest corner. They have a searchlight. To escape observation I want you to make a wide detour, say, ten miles to the northeast. Then we will bear sharp west. Our care must be not to get so far north that we shall miss the island entirely. The western shore, where the hut lies, is low.

The center of the island is high. Therefore if we come from the east our approach will be shielded. I have my compass and light. Keep bending your team to the east. When you have the right course I'll flash."

Sandy had called "Gee, Gee" three times to Ne-Nu-Ka before the direction satisfied his passenger. One of the lead dog's natural gifts was her ability to hold a straight line.

As they slithered forward, Sandy was probing his memory. Sable Island? What, if anything, did he know of it? It was sandy, desolate, uninhabited, with dwarf spruce for firewood, but no drinking water. There were two Eskimo graves at the northern tip. Fishermen and sealers often made camp there in dirty weather.

But there was more recent news. In late summer, when the light had once struck it just right, some silvery surface on the southern beach had reflected the sun and dazzled the eyes of Porcupine people. The sun had revealed the presence of bright metal on the island. It had happened only once. The next day the reflecting surface had been removed, or had been masked. That shining object, Sandy now reasoned, might have been the galvanized roof of a hut, before it had been concealed under brush or gravel.

There was also the Cree's story. Sandy wondered whether the Lieutenant had heard it. But the man was a notorious liar, and his tale had been pooh-poohed. The Cree, married to an Eskimo woman, fished with his wife's people in the summer, and trapped for the Company in the winter. He said that a low, grey boat, without flag or name, had come into the Bay at night. The men on the boat spoke English. A cousin of his wife had gone with them as guide to the islands. The guide had not returned. The Eskimos supposed that a colony had been planted somewhere in the Bay, and that their relative was remaining with it.

The dogs had been moving westward for the better part of an hour when the boy's speculations were cut short by his employer. "Pull up, Driver. Land should be right over against us. I think I saw a flash. They may have an aerial lighthouse on the blind side of the hut. Stand by your team, while I scout a bit. I can see you better than you can see me."

Within fifteen minutes the man was back. They had come within an ace of running past the island. A clump of evergreens, fifty feet in from the shore of the little harbor, was the backlog against which a monster drift had piled itself. By some caprice of the wind currents, a gully had been scoured between two sections of this drift. A baker's dozen of stunted spruce stood in the gully, and provided walls without a roof.

At the upper end of the gully Sandy established his tether line, and attached the dogs. The chains gave them scope to dig themselves in. The Lieutenant repeatedly impressed upon the boy the absolute necessity of keeping out of sight and of keeping quiet. One squint at a straying dog or one howl would give their whole show away

He was explicit also as to how he wanted the camp lay-out. "Only unpack the things we must use. Leave the komatik at the open end, headed for the water, with harness and extension line ready. We may need to snap on the dogs and pull out in a hurry. You can tie the canvas windbreak to two of the bushes. What I dread chiefly is that your dogs will sing. All dogs sing at times. We are a good mile from the hut, and in this tunnel, which is in our favor. It is barely possible that they may think the singers are wolves. But remember that from now on you have nothing on earth to do except to keep these animals quiet. Leap on the one who starts to howl, tie his jaws, strangle him, knock him cold with your brake bar, but make him hush up. There

are three good hours before light," continued the officer. "I want to discover a peek-hole, preferably in some foliage, where I can post myself during the day."

From his iron box he took a revolver, removed and examined the cartridges, slipped it into an inner pocket of his parka. He did the same with a pair of binoculars. On hands and knees, he crept to the crest of the nearest ridge. The stars gave enough illumination to work by.

"I shall not be able to see them, nor they me, until I get to the hill in the center, a half mile from here. With the drifts, the altitude must be a hundred feet," he called down to Sandy.

The boy fed his dogs, massaged their feet in his hand, one by one, as the Old Racer had coached him, examined the tie chains critically, and turned the sledge for a quick get-away. Between two scrub trees he tied the rectangle of canvas that was to screen the Lieutenant's and his head from the wind as they slept, anchoring the lower edge with chunks of snow. The rolled-up sleeping bags he used as a seat. On the spirit stove he melted snow for tea, fried bacon and ate it with a quarter loaf of his mother's bread. He opened a can of beans, and left it, together with more bacon, to be heated when his employer should return.

As he relaxed on the bed roll, the outlines of his drowsing dogs barely discernible in the starlight, Sandy felt beautifully at peace. It would soon be daylight, but how different from yesterday's dawn! Yesterday he was in the dumps, on the verge of tears because of a job that had not materialized, ashamed to meet the people to whom he owed money, despondent of ever making a go of the one business which could save him from offices and white collars. But today's sunrise would find him at work, for twenty-five dollars a day. He could settle for the hardware and the fencing. He could put Beaver square with the Old Chief and with Middle Beaver. Best of all, reliable little Sally could have her part. And there would be a dividend for Beaver and himself. Christmas was coming . . . something pretty for his mother . . . and a new pipe for his father. . . . Yes, Sir . . . every cent of it earned by their dogs . . . automatically the boy kicked the sleeping bag straight, pushed in his legs and body, laid his mittens under his head for a pillow . . . and breathed deeper, deeper.

With the murky twilight that passes for sunrise in the North, the Lieutenant glided into camp. His glance gathered in the arrangement of the dogs, who did no more than flicker snowy eyelashes at him, the sled, the sleeping boy, the bacon, bread and beans beside the spirit lamp. He lighted his pipe with the contented expression of a weary man whose affairs, nevertheless, march well. He prepared and consumed his food, and disappeared within the second sleeping bag.

From noon to three, the Lieutenant occupied his observation post. The hut, he reported, was manned by two Europeans and an Eskimo. They had a telescope, a searchlight, a guide light, masked by the north wall of the hut, for southbound aircraft. By Heaven's own luck, they had no dogs. Late in the day he screwed his electrical gadgets upon the lid of the metal trunk.

"It must be weather data that they are sending," he muttered. "Visibility, barometric readings, velocity of the wind, atmospheric pressure, temperature. Intended for some ship, or carrier, or air base; to the north, northeast or northwest. The hut is at the southernmost expanse of unguarded water. The sheet of ice before their door is an ideal take-off for a raid upon the factory cities that fringe the Great Lakes. Refuelled at this hut, there is no existing defensive opposition to stand between bombers and success. They've simply got to be smashed before they get going. We haven't much time."

He continued to talk. "Tonight I'll get closer. Into that outhouse, anyway, that smells of gasoline. You wear the head-set, Sandy. Write in this notebook. You won't understand it, but get it down. It'll be a jumble of figures and letters, but you get it down. When they finish sending you can go to bed. So long."

★ ★ ★

The dial of Sandy's watch marked eleven, and he was dead for sleep. He had caught nothing intelligible. Sandwiched between long intervals of inaction would come staccato letters and symbols. XG7. 420Y. ACW. 2 Squares; 5 Circles; 7 Dots. It was stupid work, but he had written several pages.

At the sudden pressure of a hand on his shoulder he smothered a cry. The Lieutenant was back, speaking low and earnestly.

"I'm not getting anywhere, Mackay. As soon as those blighters turn in I've got to see the inside of their diggings. I may be caught. That's the rub. Put your

watch with mine. Now; eleven hours, six minutes.
Listen carefully.

"At one o'clock you are to load the sled. I'll put my
stuff back in the box at once. Harness your team. Have
everything ready for the whistle. If I come I'll come
a-running. But if I don't come . . ." The man withdrew sheets of script from inside his shirt and wrapped
them, together with what Sandy had written, in a rub-
ber tobacco pouch. "Have you some place where you
can pin this in?"

Sandy nodded and reached for the pouch.

"At two o'clock, if I am not back, it will mean that
I am not coming back. You push off, without me. Make
a wide detour to the east, as we did in coming. They
will be looking for my party, and you don't want to be
seen. Once at Porcupine, before you unhitch your
team, deliver the tobacco pouch to Donaldson. He will
understand what to do next. These people have friends
on shore. They may communicate. Don't let anyone
stop you. Don't talk. If they shoot your dogs, run. If
you can't run, crawl. Two o'clock sharp. If I'm not
here, get going fast. Cheerio." He was mounting the
snowy incline.

★ ★ ★

Sandy pushed back his hood to hear better. The hand of his watch was moving toward the hour of two. From the other side of the central drift some minutes before, he thought that he had heard pistol shots. The team was hitched and lying down. They wanted to dig in for the night, but he kicked them awake.

One minute past two. He gave Ne-Nu-Ka's collar a tug and the komatik slid smoothly out upon the ice. That man was a prince. He hated to leave him. But his part was to obey orders. When he had put six or seven miles between himself and the island, he let Ne-Nu-Ka bear south, toward the mouth of the Abitibi. The dogs had been well-fed and without exercise for two days. This was their chance to show off. And they put all they had of muscle, lungs and heart into it.

In the lee of Crazy Squaw Island, Sandy slackened speed. A five-dog hitch, with a broad, tall driver was making for the open Bay. As Sandy was entering from the east, he had missed meeting them. They might be on their way to intercept him. He had come home faster than anyone would calculate.

The light was poor and he could not be positive, but three of the outbound dogs were surely white. What did white dogs at that river mouth signify? The only white dogs in the region, beside his own, belonged to Butcher Smok. Was Butch selling supplies to Sable Island? Was he the friend on shore, to whom the Lieutenant referred?

Sandy heard far-away shouting to the rear, but his answer was another sharp whistle to Ne-Nu-Ka. The dogs still had heart, lungs, and legs to put into their job. Nor did they slow down until Sandy dropped off the runners at Donaldson's cabin, delivered the tobacco pouch, and told his story. The policeman counted out the bills for four days' pay.

"Try to have two teams ready by Monday or Tuesday. Johnny Dolan has a second-hand sledge he'll sell cheap," were the tall man's final words. He turned the key in his lock and crossed to the telephone, unfolding the Lieutenant's papers.

9. *The Men from Headquarters*

TLEETA'S half-baked amateur team was given no rest. Of the motley pack which had been given try-outs, four were possible candidates. These and the leader were housed together and fed extra meat and meal. For four dollars they bought Dolan's old sled, and for three dollars more had contracted with Chief Beaver to cut it apart, oil the pieces, splice them where cracked, and assemble the joints with strings of new moosehide. At the Company store the boys bought blanketing to pad the collars.

From morning to night, with short rests, they worked on the five dogs, hitching them singly, in pairs, with veterans, or by themselves. The ease with which

Tleeta picked up the commands convinced them that at some era of his unknown past he had been a freight animal. They might not succeed, but they were exerting every nerve to crowd a month's training into a week.

Friday and Saturday elapsed without a summons from the policeman. But on Sunday, Beaver encountered him on the Middle Trail, where the path branches off to the back entry of Butcher Smok's store. Both were on snowshoes. Fresh snow had fallen and the Corporal, bending forward, was deciphering tracks which led to and from Smok's. Beaver might have passed unobserved had not the tall man happened to glance up, and wave his arm.

"Do you know how far up the river the ice is good?" he inquired without preliminaries.

Beaver shook his head.

"Would you mind finding out? Ulysses broadcasts with every customer who comes to the store. He may have heard. Find if it's passable as far as Flat Hand Rapids." As an afterthought he added, "How's your scrub team getting on?"

The Indian boy bunched his shoulders. "Not good, not bad. So-so."

"Well, when you find out about the ice, you and
Sandy come to my place."

Talking it over later with his partner, Beaver concluded, "He got big idea. He think Butch on Island."

The handy-man of the Company, Ulysses, as it turned out, did have a friend who had mushed down the Abitibi the preceding week. If one kept a lookout for air-holes and the overflow water at the bends, the going was good enough.

It lasted the whole evening, that discussion at the Corporal's cabin. The policeman addressed the boys as equals, for they were to take part in the new expedition, whereas he was to remain at Porcupine. While they were there, headquarters called him to the telephone several times. Details as to food and bedding were talked over and agreed upon, so far as was possible in advance.

"This time a fire will be allowed," said the Corporal, "so that you can take meal as well as fish and seal meat. There will be five men, and you will be under the orders of the officer who is in charge of the party. They will have firearms, ammunition and shovels, and a couple of heavy chests. Their aim is to capture the two white men in the hut, and to rescue their friend, if he is still alive. From your description of the Lieutenant's camp-site, you'll do well to use it again.

"The enemy will be expecting a relief party, but they will not know when or how many. I think that the baggage will be all that the two sleds can stagger under, particularly Beaver's. But the men are all hardy lads and can walk. In fact, they can lend a hand on the sleds if you strike tipped-up ice. We are keeping our preparations under cover because we believe that the Sable Islanders have connections along the shore, or even here in Porcupine. These people might side with the Island in a fight, or, at least, signal them of your departure. That is why the Chief has ordered me to stick around here, in the hope of picking up clues.

"That is also the reason why the headquarters men will not start from here. You boys are to go to Flat Hand Rapids, and make camp near the dead poplars, where the railway line runs close to the river. You are to go by daylight, so that you can note and remember any bad spots in the ice, for when you come down the river and pass Porcupine it will be night. Depending on the weather, the headquarters men will come by a motor handcar or by locomotive. But their agreed destination is the dead poplars on the big bend. Because of the unusual risk, to you and your dogs, the Chief has authorized me to warn you, and to offer you the wages of two full teams, although Beaver's is only half a team. That means fifty dollars a day for dogs and drivers, all provisions to be furnished by you. But you get the food from the Company store, and what the headquarters men eat we will pay for at the current price. You fellows had better get your bedding, provisions and teams in order tomorrow, and I will give you the word when to push off. Probably it will be noon of the day after. And I don't need to remind you that you are fools for luck, to have such an opportunity fall into your laps, right at the beginning of your dog business."

Sandy was not a great talker, and Beaver talked not at all, when he could wangle himself out of it. Neither of them said more than "thanks Corporal" and shook hands. Nor did they need to exchange confidences as they walked homeward along Three-Mile Trail. Each knew the thoughts of the other. Beaver put their common anxiety into words when, at the schoolhouse corner, he turned into the spruce thicket toward his father's lodge.

"Second dogs need big run tomorrow. Must learn fast."

★ ★ ★

The exhaust of a motor handcar echoed through the gorge of Flat Hand Rapids. Five men tumbled stiffly to the ground, tying on their snowshoes. They were vigorous young fellows and their clothing showed them to be adept in the art of protecting themselves against the northern winter. Shouldering their bulky material, they crossed the two hundred yards that separated the railway line from the stream. They had rifles, the dismounted sections of a rapid-fire gun, and ammunition for both. In a gingerly handled wooden box were twenty-four hand grenades. Sandy gaped at three short-handled shovels. Were they going to farm on Sable Island? They brought no food and their personal baggage was limited to waterproofed sleeping sacks.

The boys had left the komatiks on the ice, with the pack ropes undone, and while the man who seemed to be in command, and whom the others addressed as Captain, supervised the loading, Sandy put the final touches to breakfast. The Corporal had warned him that the men would have been travelling throughout the bitter night and would be ferociously hungry. Sandy had pilot biscuit, marmalade and tea, ham and fried potatoes, with plenty of everything.

"Good boys," smiled the Captain, sniffing the perfume of the ham. They squatted under the lee of the canvas wind break and ate and ate and ate.

"As we got no sleep last night," said the Captain, "and will be on the move again tonight, we'll lie doggo until four o'clock. If you boys will have a meal at that hour, and the teams hitched, we will get under way. And after this breakfast, as a sample of what you can do, I propose that you fellows do the cooking on this trip, and our crowd will take on the cleaning up."

Sandy glanced at Beaver and said, "It's a trade, Sir." The look of understanding between the partners meant that one of them would be feeding the dogs while the other was feeding the humans.

On Sandy's sledge they lashed the food and cooking utensils, the dogs chains and shovels, the canvas shelter, the machine gun and the ammunition. On Beaver's was the bedding, the hand grenades and the rifles, a bundle of dry kindling and the axe. For convenience in handling, all the small articles had been stowed in flour sacks. As the loads were only moderately heavy for traction over ice, two of the headquarters men could ride, taking turns with those who would walk or trot alongside. Beaver was vastly relieved by the arrangement, for it meant that he could run beside Tleeta. This way his dogs would give no trouble. Their one idea would be to crowd up on the first team, like kindergarten children who are afraid of being left behind.

Porcupine was shrouded in a bank of cold vapor, as they trotted past at ten o'clock. Sandy fancied that a tall, dark figure was on the ice, a little out from the shore. But it gave no signal. It might have been Donaldson. It might have been Butch. More probably, it was the boy's imagination.

"I'd better quit seeing things that aren't there," he scolded himself.

Once clear of the mainland, Sandy checked the teams and described the Lieutenant's route to the Captain.

"Do just as he did," ordered the latter. "And I don't think that we can do better—for our initial base, anyway—than to make camp at his harbor."

Early on the route, Ne-Nu-Ka caught the idea that she was returning to the gully which had recently been her home. After that she required no further guidance. Sandy marvelled afresh at the instinct which pilots a dog to the locality he has previously known.

Nothing indicated that the Lieutenant's camp-site had been disturbed or even visited. With many hands to divide the work, the two strings of dogs were soon staked out, the firearms loaded, the bedding unrolled, and the men asleep. Woodcutting and cooking would wait for daylight. Beaver and Sandy still moved among their teams, distributing slabs of fish, feeling their feet, making sure of collars and fastenings. Although he did not believe that their approach had been observed, the Captain nevertheless posted a guard.

After breakfast the Captain decided to try a small experiment. With a brushwood stick between his teeth, he crawled on hands and knees to the ridge of the central hill. Upon the stick he hoisted his cap a few inches above the ridge. Two shots rang out. The Captain let himself slide back into the gully.

"That's that," he said grimly. "They mean to fight. And they must have telescopic sights. I could feel the wind of their bullets."

For ten minutes the leader smoked, deep in thought, then called his men together.

"Huddle round, fellows. Yes, and you boys, too. You are in this with us. Since seeing the layout of the island, a scheme has occurred to me that may clean out that hornet's nest. My orders are to bring home those men dead or alive, and to rescue our Lieutenant, unless he has already been killed. What we do must be done quickly. The men in that hut have probably radioed their base that they have been attacked. A party to re-inforce them may be near. Or, they may be set to execute their raid on the Lake cities, today, tonight, or tomorrow. If that is so they will jam it through regardless. It's got to be smashed, or we shall be too late.

"The strategy I now propose has three distinct elements. I will explain these three sections, one by one, in detail. Every one of you, even the dogs, has a vital part in them. You may see objections to the plan. If so, save them until I have finished.

"Now for the first section. Beginning immediately, I want you four headquarters men to start tunnelling into that central drift. We can assume a snow depth of fifteen to twenty-five feet. The drift has been packed by heavy wind, and there is a good crust. Ten feet below the highest point start digging. Once you have passed the high point of the hill, dig on a downward incline. The tunnel should continue seventy-five feet past the crest. From then on, we can make it a zigzag trench, which will go faster. As we shall be working three or four feet below the top level of the snow, and on the bias, the enemy will have nothing to aim at. From the hut they will see snow being pitched into the air, but no men.

"When we get within hurling distance, we will throw grenades against the building. Not many, but enough to demonstrate that we can demolish their tin fort at will. We must convince them that they are the rats in the trap. It would be swell if one of our grenades could knock out their generator. But we do not want to injure the Lieutenant, whom we may suppose is inside, gagged and helpless.

"I repeat the first of the three sections of our tactic. You four men are alone in it. You get to digging at once. Three dig and one stand sentry, keeping the four rifles ready. Here is a periscope, which the sentry will have charge of, and give warning of a sortie. I do not think that they will venture outside the hut. If they do, you have rifles, and four men out to repulse two. If no mishap occurs, we should be within grenade distance of the hut around four o'clock tomorrow morning, and have finished with the grenades by five. At noon, at sundown, and at midnight Sandy and Beaver will take food to the tunnel.

"The second section of my strategy concerns Beaver and his five dogs—them alone. It is a solo performance, with the boy and his team the only actors. It will require nerve on your part, Beaver, but you are the only member of our party who stands a chance of pulling it off. Pay attention, and you, Sandy, translate if he gets muddled. We are assuming that the two men in the hut will have their confidence shaken by the explosions on the roof and against the wall. They will know that they are outnumbered. They will not know what further offensive weapon we are holding in reserve. They will be figuring to destroy evidence of their plot, and to save their skins, when upon the scene appears an unarmed Indian boy and a team of dogs, coming from the northwest. To wait in their hut means death, but Beaver may tempt them to make a dash for life. They may reason that it is a ten-to-one chance, but don't forget that they have an Eskimo who can handle dogs, and guide them to a hide-out.

"What, concretely, is Beaver's action? As soon as one more hour's work will finish the trench, Beaver and his dogs, with an empty sledge, will pass around the north cape of the island, and proceed in a northwesterly direction for an hour and a half. Then he will stop and wait. Light begins to filter through shortly before eight o'clock. At daylight he will lay a straight course for the hut. With their first morning view of the ice, the men who have just been badly shaken up with grenades, will see an Indian boy, with an empty sled, unarmed, coming to them from the northwest. Beaver had better run beside his leader, not to come too fast. The hut men will have no reason to associate this Indian with the trench-diggers and the grenade-throwers. He will seem a providential coincidence, too good not to take advantage of. They may even suppose that he has been sent by their friends.

"Get this straight, Beaver. You are to stop your team three hundred feet from the hut. Throw back your hood, so that they can be sure you are an Indian. Hold up your hand, palm outward, to show that you are unarmed. After this pantomime, you will stand quietly by Tleeta. The next move is up to the men of the hut. I can't imagine that they will shoot at you. If they do, make yourself scarce, and work your way back to camp. If the Eskimo takes your dogs, let him have them. He will drive north. You go with them but you drop behind before they get to the north end of the Island. Do you understand this, Beaver?"

Without change of expression, the Indian boy nodded. "Me understood."

The Captain now addressed himself to Sandy. "The third element of our plan concerns you, your team, the machine gunner and myself. The reason I am entering into all this detail is because our campaign is a three-ring circus. All rings will be performing at the same time. I want each player in each ring to know precisely what his fellow-actors are doing. After we have thrown our grenades, three men will remain in the trench, watching their chance to rescue the Lieutenant. Beaver will be out in front, tempting the enemy to use his team for a getaway. Sandy, the gunner and myself will be at the north cape prepared to take pot shots at the refugees when they draw within range. Should the machine gun not stop them, the gunner and myself will use Sandy's faster team to overhaul them.

"I want to say to you boys right now, we know you set store by your animals. If any of them get shot in this mix-up, as seems possible, we will do our best to make it right. We men would be hog-tied without the help of your teams.

"Now, before we start digging, has anyone a question?" The Captain looked hard into the six serious faces. "Right-o," he said, rising. "Get your shovels and rifles."

The day had turned out fine. The fog had dispersed, and there was little wind. The sun, like a dingy orange, was poised above the southern horizon. There was little chance of snow.

At noon, when Sandy carried up the corned-beef hash and beans, the tunnel was twenty-five feet beyond the ridge. The short handles and steel blades made play of the digging. But what held up progress was the tiresome job of carrying the excavated snow to the tunnel mouth. While they ate, Sandy inspected their progress.

"Why not let me bring up a strip of the canvas that covers the sled?" he queried. "You can throw snow right on it, like loading a flatcar. It is frozen stiff and will slide like tin. We can reeve hand-holds through the eyelets to haul it by."

The headquarters men looked sheepish. "Fine idea, kid. We never thought of that," said one. "For that matter why not have two strips of canvas? The shovellers can be loading the second strip while the third man hauls away the loaded one."

The sentinel, as Sandy waited for him to empty his plate, let the latter peer into the periscope. It was the boy's first view of the much-talked-of hut.

"It isn't a hut at all," he exclaimed. "It's a beautiful house."

To Sandy "hut" signified walls of undressed stone,

which the Eskimos or Indians piled together without mortar. But this was a cottage of galvanized iron, with glass windows and several rooms. The iron roof was concealed with brush, held in place by wire and rocks. Even at the distance of a hundred and fifty feet he could hear the purr of an electric motor.

During the afternoon the boys fed and brushed the dogs, working a drop of bacon fat between their toes, and greased the harness. Luxury of this sort is not within the routine of freight dogs, but the boys were subconsciously affected by the excitement of the Captain's enterprise and could not sit idle. Anyway, it civilized the dogs, and made them more easily handled. As they brushed they discussed the probability of the Lieutenant being alive.

"If they have tortured him, I wouldn't like to be in their boots when the Captain gets his hands on them," commented Sandy.

Beaver's lips were a thin copper line.

10. *The Fight on the Ice*

DURING daylight, and now for twelve hours of polar starlight, the men had persisted doggedly in their tunnelling and trenching. A few hundred more shovelfuls and their corkscrew canal would be fifty feet from the goal. At that distance grenades would be effective.

The inaction within the hut worried the Captain. Had they a depth bomb or poison gas that they would discharge without warning against his little party? Or would the hut be blown to smithereens, the moment an invader set foot upon the threshold? During the day the inmates had indulged in target practice at the tip of the periscope, but since nightfall, nothing. The hut was in darkness, nor had they turned the searchlight upon the trench.

Had the Captain but known it, the men in the hut awaited his attack complacently. They felt amply able to repel any force he might bring against them. While the headquarters men were feverishly burrowing in the snow, inside the hut one of the Europeans was sorting and burning papers, the other was repairing a magneto, and the Eskimo was erecting a barricade of planks. They were expecting a rough-and-tumble onslaught with fists, revolvers and rifles. The spearhead, they believed, must inevitably be directed against the front door.

The door was solid oak, the windows were fitted with iron shutters, the walls were of double metal sheeting, the roof was bullet and fireproof. Just inside the door four parallel strips of brass were screwed to the floor. These were charged with two thousand volts. The hero who battered in the door and stepped inside would wilt in his tracks. Indeed, the men of the hut felt assuredly competent to defend themselves, and to administer a fatal lesson to snoopers who came prying where they were not wanted. They already had one of them, trussed and frozen, in the gasoline storehouse, and would willingly give others a dose of the same medicine. On a counter behind the barricade reposed four repeating rifles for each defender. Extra clips were neatly stacked. Should an invader escape electrocution at the entrance it would be like pigeon shooting to finish him off. They had unquestioning confidence in the impregnable security of their flanks and rear.

Behind the hut the final shovelful of snow was tossed from the trench. The wooden box of grenades was tenderly opened.

"Each take one and all heave together." The Captain's voice was tense and sibilant. "Two of you try for the roof where the stovepipe emerges. The other two aim at the rear wall. I'll have a shy at the barred window. Hold down the lever. Pull the pin. Ready! Throw!"

The detonation was prodigious. On the roof, the bushes were blown away and four sheets of corrugated iron were wrenched from their bolts. In the rear wall seams were opened in the sheathing wide enough for the passage of a man's body. The lock of the window shutter was blasted off, and the two halves of the shutter swung drunkenly outward, leaving the wooden sash exposed.

The Captain was as excited as a boy at the success of the first stage of his strategy.

"I can't resist one more attempt," he whispered. "Under the window is the diesel generator, where the exhaust sticks out. The Lieutenant won't be confined among the machinery."

He balanced the lemon-shaped missile of cast iron in his hand. This time he did not toss the grenade underhand, but hurled it like a pitched ball. There was a roar, a flash, and the hum of machinery stopped.

"The moral effect of carrying the battle to their mechanized equipment will be excellent," the Captain laughed. "Now we shall let them stew in their own thoughts for a while. You fellows rest, until the bait trots into sight. Beaver ought to be somewhere eating his lunch, waiting for daybreak. I needn't warn you chaps, when you do get into the house, to be on the lookout for lighted fuses, charged wires, chemicals and gas. Watch where you step. Don't touch metal. It's the Lieutenant we want first. He'll be in a bad way, poor fellow, in some corner. The gunner, Sandy and I must get on with our part of the show. You have your rifles and automatics. So long."

The two men and their grenade box, returning to

camp, found Sandy hard put to keep his dogs from stampeding. To them explosions meant hunting, game, with delicious warm meat at the end.

"This makes a slight change in our plan," said the Captain to the gunner. "I had thought that we might lash the machine gun on the komatik. But if shooting makes the dogs jumpy, you never could aim. We will set up your machine among the evergreens near the beach, and leave the team hidden behind the point until we actually need it for pursuit. We can only hope and pray that the Eskimo drives close inshore."

Starlight was by now dwindling into dawn, and by the faint light an indistinct group could be seen coming in from the center of the Bay. On closer view it was a driver running beside an empty sledge, his dogs at a a brisk trot. A hundred yards from the cabin he came to a stop, threw back his hood and upraised empty hands. There were no shots or other indications of interest from the hut. The Indian stood motionless, his hand on the lead dog's head. Now was the critical moment, with everything hanging in the balance.

Abruptly the door of the hut was thrown wide. An Eskimo, rifles on his arm, bounded toward the sledge, followed by two white men. One of the pair limped and his companion boosted him over the uneven ice on the beach. The Europeans threw themselves upon the sledge, the Eskimo shouted to the dogs, gestured to Beaver to fall behind, and set a northerly course under the lee of the land.

The men of the trench, running to the house, found smoke pouring from the doorway.

The runaways, to safeguard their own exit, had pulled the switches, and to destroy evidence of their aerial preparations had heaped their papers on the floor, thrown mattresses and boxes upon them, splashed the pile with gasoline, and applied a match. The boxes and straw were ablaze, but the flames had not as yet had time to descend to the documents. With their mittened hands the headquarters men pitched boxes and mattresses out of doors. Peeling off their woolen mackinaws, they smothered what fire remained. Had the men been two minutes later the interior of the hut would have been a furnace.

Then began a systematic search for the Lieutenant. In the cupboards, the bunks, the storeroom, under the flooring, even in the open loft was no sign of their comrade, no reply to their calls.

"The poor chap isn't here," they admitted soberly. "They've murdered him and hid the body in the snow."

"But what about the smaller building?" asked one.

They forced the padlock. Inside were forty drums of aviation gasoline, of fifty gallons each, and stretched upon them, barely breathing, was the Lieutenant. His wrists and ankles were bound with wire. A length of fuse made plain the grewsome method by which they had intended to destroy supplies and prisoner, both with a single match, had the grenades not upset their equilibrium, and had the empty dog sled not prompted them to precipitate flight.

The escaping Europeans made good time. The Eskimo, like all of his race, knew how to make the most of a team of Malemutes. To escape the wind he drove close to shore. The passengers, looking back and seeing no effort at pursuit, breathed easier. Suddenly to their shocked ears came the stutter of a rapid-fire gun, from a patch of foliage near the point. The first spray of bullets passed high overhead, an invitation to halt and capitulate. But the white men were not the sort who surrender. At the sound of shooting the Eskimo had thrown himself flat upon the ice, as Little Beaver, lagging behind, did also. The team, driverless, continued to gallop forward. The passengers were raising their rifles.

"You'll have to drop a couple of the dogs," muttered the Captain. "We can't let the sled get out of range."

The gunner lowered his sights, squeezed the grip. Tleeta and the first swing sagged in their tracks. The willing creatures made an effort to keep on, but faltered and fell. Without hesitation the two men had rolled from the sled, and rested their gun barrels upon it. They intended a fight to the finish.

The Captain wrinkled his forehead. "They force us to do it. Shoot the men."

The gunner sprayed a stream of bullets back and forth, twice, as one plays the nozzle of a garden hose. The heads of the two men relaxed forward, faces down. Moko and Ittycut, the surviving dogs, terrified by the unusual noises, clawed desperately, dragging the sledge and the bodies of their team-mates a dozen paces. With the support of the sled removed, the two Europeans flopped inertly to the ice.

The Captain came into the open and shouted rearward. "Oh you, Sandy. The war's over. Bring your team around to this side."

Leaving the gunner to dismount his machine, he picked his way down the beach. He was within forty feet of the bodies when one of them stirred and came to a sitting position, drawing a revolver from the breast of his jacket. The man's eyes were glazing, he was weak from loss of blood, the arm holding the pistol swayed from side to side. But his lips were set in a snarl of hate. He was concentrating every ounce of his ebbing strength into that dying shot.

Whether he would have hit the Captain will never be known. Floating across the ice, airy as a leaf riding the wind, a stumpy figure flung itself at the European's revolver arm. Beaver and the expiring man gripped and floundered. But by that time it was the Captain who held the weapon. The Eskimo submitted to handcuffs without a struggle.

The Captain had fulfilled his mission. The bodies of the men of Sable Island would be brought home, the Lieutenant was rescued. But there remained a score of secondary matters to put in order. The Lieutenant's hands and feet had been painfully frost-bitten, and much of the time his mind wandered. For the past three days, since they had become convinced that he would give no information, his captors had abandoned him, without food or drink, to the cold of the gasoline store-house. The Lieutenant's physical fitness was all that had kept him alive. His friends made a shakedown before the stove of the hut, and the Captain detailed a man as nurse. Two other men were assigned the task of classifying and boxing the papers that were left.

The Captain now determined to transfer the camp from the gully to the building. Although the boys said little, they grieved sincerely over the loss of Tleeta and his mates. Beaver's small team had hardly been trained before it was wrecked. Each of them had a lump in his throat, as they unbuckled the harness, and prepared to bury the poor creatures.

"It's not worth the trouble of burying them in the snow. The wolves will have them out before we leave. It feels more decent, though," said Sandy thoughtfully.

"You wait." Beaver had an idea. Bringing the axe, he chopped an opening in the ice. With stones from the beach they weighted the bodies, and let them slide into the transparent depth. "Wolf no eat Tleeta now," said Beaver. Thus closed the checkered career of the tawny, hard-working ex-cannibal.

"Who knows," reflected Sandy, "but that the old fellow's death prevented the injury or death of one of our men."

With the sick Lieutenant and the bodies of the two Europeans to portage, plus the arsenal and records of the hut, plus the original camp equipment, all the men would need to make the return trip on foot. But instead of overloading the team, and attempting to take all the goods at once, it seemed more sensible for Sandy to plan for an additional trip later in the week. The Captain therefore appointed a man to remain at the hut as guardian. Much of the machinery was valuable. One never knew who might be nosing about, particularly as persons on the mainland were suspected of being in sympathy with the islanders.

Among the items salvaged from the fire, were three thousand dollars in new five-dollar bills. While no allusion to Butcher Smok appeared in the records, in the storeroom was a quantity of canned food and cigars, of the brands which Butch alone had for sale in the Hudson Bay territory.

The Europeans, being dead, could impart no information. But the Eskimo could and did talk. A lead-colored ship, claiming to be a fisherman, with officers who spoke English, was wintering in an inlet of Ungava Bay. The ship was hard to distinguish from its background, for the crew had removed the masts and banked the deck with snow. This news interested the Captain to such a degree that he made but a momentary halt at Porcupine, before driving his motor handcar back to headquarters, with the native, and the maps which proved that the bombing project was no myth.

The Lieutenant was installed at the Corporal's to recuperate, where good Mother Swain, Porcupine's nearest approach to a doctor, could practice the efficacy of her herb garden upon him. The Captain engaged himself to send a locomotive and snow plow for the invalid, the four men, and the mass of material, as soon as Sandy should have ferried it ashore.

Five days later, as Beaver, Sandy, and the guard were quitting the island for the last time, a plane, northbound, skimmed among the clouds. An Eskimo, as passenger, was advising the navigator. After many hours of uninterrupted flight the native was able to distinguish a fishing smack, frozen in for the winter. The flying officer diminished altitude to investigate. Two planes were being assembled on the deck and on the adjacent icefloe. A broadside from anti-aircraft guns punctured a wing of the plane. In view of these facts the flyer felt justified in dropping two bombs upon the masquerading fisherman.

The result was devastating. The ship must have been carrying a full cargo of explosives. The visitor idled about, for the smoke to dissipate. Where the ship had been nothing remained but a circle of blue-black water.

A discreet number of weeks elapsed before the exploit of the Captain, the Lieutenant, and the bomber was released to the radio and the newspapers. But one evening Corporal Don, listening dutifully as was his custom each evening, heard the electrifying message.

"Without stating the date or the locality," the announcer was saying, "it can be authoritatively made public that an enemy plot to bomb the metal and manu-

facturing district of the Great Lakes has been discovered and smashed, as it was on the point of being
carried into effect. Planes and ammunition had actually
been smuggled into the Dominion. A re-fueling station
was in readiness within easy striking distance of the
world's greatest automobile city. A post for signaling
atmospheric conditions was functioning. In addition
to the heroic work of the officers who apprehended
the enemy agents, the authorities wish to acknowledge
the aid furnished by the drivers and teams of the Hudson Bay Express."

It was an intensely cold night, but the Corporal
wormed into his furs and tramped up to the Factory.
Sandy and Little Beaver were out back, giving extra
bedding to a new litter of pups. At the news, Beaver,
on one of the rare instances of his lifetime, showed his
teeth in a smile. Sandy was jubilant.

"This puts us on the map, doesn't it, Corporal? If
the papers print our name, a lot of business will be coming our way. The Captain and the Lieutenant said
they'd recommend us, too."

Corporal Donaldson opened his mouth to speak.
"I . . . I . . . that is . . . I . . ." The old drill
master was actually tongue-tied with modesty. "That

is . . . the assistant commissioner has telephoned to notify me of my promotion. That business of Sable Island has made a stir. I suppose I should have been pleased. . . ."

"You not go," growled Beaver. "No, not go."

"It would be a terrible thing, to have you leave Porcupine now," said Sandy. "We were counting on working on your tough cases. Please decide not to go away."

"No," admitted the policeman, rubbing his toothbrush moustache. "I thanked him, but I'm not leaving. Of course I like to be near you boys. But I have a private reason." He lowered his voice. "I haven't caught up with Butch yet. He left his house the same night they captured the Lieutenant on the island. He hasn't been heard from since, except that word has got around that his business is for sale. Some of the five-dollar bills of that series will turn up, if we are patient. Sly as he is, Butch will stub his toe some fine day. I'm staying on here to help him do it."

11. *A Place for Quicksilver*

THE WORK that had begun as a stopgap, a filler-in for idle time, a provisional meal ticket, as it were, had become the main activity of the partners' business.

Of course they were always on call to bring stranded or injured people to the train, the doctor, or the hospital at Cochrane; to aid protégés of Father Antoine, or to further detective inquiries of the Corporal. Theoretically, Donaldson was a member of the Mounted Police. But as a horse would have been more of a hindrance than a help on most of his journeys, he was obliged to rely upon his own long legs, plus canoes in summer, and skates, snowshoes, and dogs in winter.

The boys once hauled the tractor in from Rupert's House, where it had stripped its gears. And when a woods-queer half breed, jealous of Johnny's prowess in snaring white foxes, stole the Dolan baby, they clung to the trail of the kidnapper like bloodhounds for seven days, until the little girl was recovered and the crazed law-breaker had flung himself over a cliff. For such emergencies the partners were ready and willing to drop everything. But commissions of this nature were far between and often done without pay.

Every business, if it is to meet its bills, must have some steady, day-in-day-out income, and in the boys' case this income came from the freighting of gold ore. As a result of the Sable Island affair they had made the acquaintance of three brothers, mining prospectors, who were opening a vein of ore twenty-two miles west of Porcupine depot. In summer the route to their mine, intersected by wallows of bottomless muskeg, was impassable. The miners, therefore, before a company should be organized and the heavy expense of building a branch railroad undertaken, were transporting their ore to the existing railhead during the winter by dogs. As soon as the summer schedule was in operation, the accumulated ore would be loaded upon flatcars, and shipped to the stamp mill at Bluestone. The ore assayed several hundred dollars a ton, or it could never have justified the expense.

Sandy and Little Beaver had bought a Labrador toboggan, and upon this contrivance of rounded oak stringers had erected a box, like the body of a farm wagon. With the miners' help they put in a tough week, rooting out snags and stumps from the rougher sections of the mine-to-depot route. The hauling was helped by the fact that the trail to the depot was slightly downhill. With fifteen dogs they could haul a ton, or somewhat more if weather and footing favored. The miners paid eighteen dollars a ton. After experimenting, the boys had worked out a routine of three trips per week. The first day they would drive empty to the mine and take on a load. The second day they would return to the depot, weigh and discharge the load.

On alternate days, when the boys would be absent, Bumbly Bill's Sally trudged up from the station night and morning. She was only a girl, but she could be trusted to feed exactly as instructed, to have an eye on the puppies, and to give first aid to any animal who might be nipped in the interminable bickering. She fully earned her seventy-five cents a day.

The freighting of ore was just plain, unexciting hard work. But it provided money to pay Chief Beaver for seal meat, to pick up a good dog when one pleased their fancy, and to add to their savings in John Mackay's safe. Beside that, it kept dogs and drivers as hard as nails. It is doubtful whether so physically sound a freight-handling aggregation had ever been put together in the North Country.

That ore-carrying season, however, was chiefly memorable because of an accident. Rather it was the accidental discovery of something they already possessed, and few strokes of blind luck have had more long-term consequences.

For some months the partners had been aware that Ne-Nu-Ka must be retired. In the beginning she was their whole dog business. Through her pups she had given them the team. But now the boys were learning, as other dog teamsters have learned before and since, that with a heavy-working string of big, veteran draught animals, a female does not have sufficient authority for leadership. With her sensitiveness to the will of her driver, her cunning in a fight, her instinct for direction and ice, her obedience and intelligence, Ne-Nu-Ka had been a peerless individual performer.

While the team was green and young, while the first three swings were her own pups, she was irreproachable. But Ne-Nu-Ka had been far from young when the Old Racer died. And, as a clinching argument, she was about to have another family. She would be promoted to an honored old age, with the freedom of the Factory, and a box of straw under Sandy's workbench.

The boys had been trying to decide upon her successor. They had thirty-eight adult dogs, including five fair-to-middling potential leaders. Itchy-Koula, Nanuk, Kolma, Nanutuk, and Jaksut would improve with schooling, but they somehow lacked the spark, the initiative, that marks the true leader. In their trips to the mine Sandy was trying them out, in rotation.

The new leader discovered himself, elected himself, just danced in and stole the show. And he was the most improbable candidate of the whole outfit—none other than the playboy, Quicksilver, runt of the first litter. Too small to work, he had passed much of his time as the pet and companion of human beings.

Quicksilver's appearance always provoked smiles. He was black as soot, save for the white star and the quivering pink nose. Except for his miniature size, his unusual color, and his nose, which should have been black, he was the ideal conformation of the Alaskan Malemute. Erect ears soft as chamois skin, flat skull, short back, square body on firm legs, waterproof coat with thick inner wool, tail with a curl in the end. Whereas the standard weight for the breed is eighty pounds, Quicksilver, even when he was in his prime, never weighed more than forty-six pounds. But his brain was almost human. He had hob-nobbed with people so much that in ordinary domestic matters he thought along with them. With no formal training himself, he had nevertheless been exposed to the education of several relays of workers. He would sit on the sidelines and watch, sniffing impatiently through his ridiculous nose, as though to show that he knew what it was all about.

On the morning of the lucky accident, Sandy had neglected to shut in the playboy when the team departed. Kolma was having his turn as leader. Three miles out from the Factory the team was plodding solemnly mineward, when up bounced Quicksilver, pleased as Punch. He skipped lightly alongside his friends, inviting them to play, then took his station beside Kolma, who, being leader, had no partner. There he stayed.

The toboggan was on a part of the trail known as the Pig's Tail, because it was narrow and twisty. Sandy was continually shouting commands—"Gee, Haw, Gee." Quicksilver not only obeyed, but pushed Kolma in the right direction. Then, quitting his self-imposed task at the front, he ran up and down the line, stirring up the laggards, making a pretense of nipping their heels if they shirked.

Sandy did not believe his eyes. The dog was a foreman, bossing his gang! The boy had never seen a like exhibition of brains and initiative. The truth broke upon him gradually. The runts of the White Phantom-Ne-Nu-Ka litters, the Old Racer had known, were small of body but of phenomenal temperament. The driver sat on the toboggan, hypnotized. He was watching the work of one of the fabulous dogs, of which tales are told, around camp-fires, in igloos, and wigwams—A LOOSE LEADER. He was watching the dog in a hundred thousand practicing his profession. Then and there he tied Quicksilver at Kolma's side. Within a week the black midget had out-jockeyed all five rivals for the grade of top sergeant. The runt had come into his own.

★ ★ ★

A busy and uneventful summer came and went. The partners had contracted for another season with the three brothers. But neither Beaver nor Sandy was contented. They were just plain bored. The solid winter of profitable business ahead did not stir a flicker of satisfaction. They felt imprisoned. They were prosperous, to be sure. As equipment they owned new buildings, a good supply of food, a seine and two dories, two koma-

tiks, two heavy-duty Labrador toboggans, harnesses and dogs, and yet with this considerable material, they were restless. An ingredient to the happiness of fifteen-year-old boys was lacking. Nowhere in the program was novelty or adventure. With what they considered

the world's two best hitches of dogs, they wanted to do something more exhilarating than cart rocks.

This was still their mood when a telegram from Chicago arrived. It came over the railroad wire to Bumbly Bill and Sally delivered it. The Mackays were at dinner, and Sally seated herself before a saucer of pudding, her eyes sparkling. She knew what was in the wire.

Hudson Bay Express. Porcupine.

My husband Professor Rigby Armitage botanical explorer classifying arctic flora entered Lindsay Inlet with small party April fifteenth intended reaching Hudson Bay and proceeding south stop no news nine months believed perished or wintering Eskimo settlement four hundred miles north of you stop desire organize immediate search stop offer you twenty-five dollars per day plus rations team and driver stop can you engage experienced guide stop if accept meet me Cochrane soonest possible wire collect Hotel Majestic Chicago

Ann Armitage

A hush fell upon the room as the yellow paper passed from hand to hand. Sandy's lip trembled. His eyes were mutely begging his father.

John Mackay did not express himself at once. As was his habit, he was balancing the pros and cons of the situation.

"If the professor is dead, it is too late. If he is with friendly natives he will survive until spring anyway, and it will be a waste of money. But that is the lady's affair. The severest weather will soon be behind us, but the most dangerous ice is ahead. A good man must take charge. It's a fair offer, my boy. Do as you think best."

"I accept," said Sandy quickly. "But who can we get to guide the trip? He must know the country and speak Eskimo. If he doesn't know the ways of those cranky folks they'll shut up like clams. What about Chief Beaver?"

"Too old," replied John Mackay. "I'd rather have a half-breed than a full Indian. This calls for a seasoned man of forty. However, we don't have to decide today."

"But I can send the wire, can't I?" pursued the boy, going to the chimney-shelf where pen and paper were kept. The reply that he handed Sally for transmission read:

> *Accept conditions meet you Cochrane station March second*
>
> *Sandy Mackay*

The date which he had named would allow him four days to arrange his affairs, overhaul his gear, and three days to cover the two hundred and twenty miles to the winter railhead.

Few phenomena are more mystifying than the speed with which news spreads, even in the wilderness. The next afternoon warm-hearted Mother Swain, godmother to the ailing of all colors, called on Sandy's mother. The only hope of prolonging the life of the grandmother of the Panther family was to get her to the hospital for an operation. Sandy was such an obliging boy, and as he was going anyway, would he mind taking the venerable squaw? Sandy good-naturedly consented.

The priest, Pere Antoine, sent a special runner from Mainmast. Two children had lost their parents under pitiable circumstances. He was forwarding them to Mrs. Mackay the following day, for the boys to deliver at the Orphanage of the Good Shepherd. Sandy took it with philosophy. As they were travelling light, and were being paid for their time, he was glad to do a few good turns on the side. But he remarked to Beaver, "I figured on making this a speed trial, but we'll be an ambulance. You nurse the passengers and I'll nurse the dogs."

The morning of their departure, as soon as he had said the blessing at breakfast, John Mackay re-opened the subject of a guide.

"Since you and the team will be under his orders, a lot depends upon choosing the right man. Oscar Bird-seed is sober, the right age, well experienced up in that country. Before he took to trapping he was mail courier for the Company. We let him go because of his ugly temper. But if the lady will pay six dollars a day, which is more than his traps are earning, it ought to keep him on good behavior. If you think well of it, while you are away I'll get word to Oscar and have him here for her to interview. By the way, how long do you expect to be gone?"

Sandy laid down his fork. "Daylight is getting stronger. Suppose we average forty miles a day. Some days we will make twice that, but we may be storm-bound. And suppose we have a thousand miles to cover. I thought we'd take grub for thirty days. That is for the big trip. Going to Cochrane to meet the lady, with these three helpless passengers, Beaver will go along. We will spend the nights at Candlestick, Lovely Lady, and Sawtooth, where we have friends. It will save time not to make camp. If Oscar is here, say in six days, he and the lady can look one another over. She is to be his employer, you know, same as she is mine."

"Agreed," assented the Factor. There was pride in his eyes as he regarded his fifteen-year-old son. The boy knew what he was about. He governed his actions with sense and foresight. If forced into it, he would take risks, but he would know that they were risks.

With fifteen dogs, well-fed and picked for speed, and a lightly-burdened sledge, the journey to the winter terminus of the railway was hardly more than a pleasure jaunt. The boys and their protégés slept on the floors of hospitable cabins each night, and ate hot food without the drudgery of chopping wood, melting snow for water, and contriving a shelter.

It was not yet noon of March second, the date Sandy had fixed, when the team trotted into Cochrane. But Mrs. Armitage was already pacing up and down the depot platform. The boy ran across the street and paid his respects.

"We'll be right back, as soon as we leave our passengers at the Orphanage and the hospital."

The lady looked annoyed. She had a reply upon the tip of her tongue, but thought better of it, and nodded sourly. She was displeased, that was plain. Short of stature, somewhere in her early thirties, her mouth was an index to a character which would leave no expedient untried in accomplishing what she set out to do.

12. The Lady and the Guide

DRESSED sensibly in heavy trousers, her only luggage a single valise, Mrs. Armitage impressed the partners favorably. She did not seem talkative, which they liked even better. As soon as the dogs had been unharnessed and tied in the hotel stable, she led the way to the dining room for lunch. She was energetic and to the point, although she did not smile easily.

"Who were those people you were carting about this morning, while you kept me waiting on that freezing platform?" she began as she took her seat.

"They were two children of Father Antoine's, and a Cree woman of Mother Swain's," replied Sandy readily.

"Did you bring them all the way from Porcupine?" she continued.

"Yes, lady, from Porcupine to Cochrane," answered the boy.

"Well, we might as well understand one another at once. I am a business woman. When you work for me, you work for me. And for nobody else. This is the fourth day since you left Porcupine. Do you count on me to pay the wages of dogs and two drivers during the four days you were carrying passengers for Mr. Antoine and Mrs. Swain? Or did you think that I wouldn't see you sneaking into town, so that you could collect from both them and me? I call that cheating. And I am sorry to get that impression of you at our first meeting."

Sandy was stunned. No one had ever talked to him in this tone, or questioned his honesty before. He had more than his share of pride. He and Beaver had been to no end of trouble, feeding the orphans and keeping the sick squaw warm, with no thought of being paid for it. This outsider had the people of the Trapland all wrong. Perhaps he should have explained; that was the moment for it, if ever. But the words wouldn't come. It would seem like apologizing. He was numb with anger, to the soles of his feet, and merely scowled into his napkin.

Unfortunately Mrs. Armitage was a lady who didn't know when to stop.

"I don't suppose that Mr. Antoine and Mrs. Swain are paupers. You can look to them for your pay. You start working for me as of today noon. And I hope this may be a lesson to you."

With this unhappy introduction, the meal proceeded and finished in silence. The partners and their employer were off to a bad start.

"And I don't mind telling you another thing," Mrs. Armitage added, as she laid down her napkin. "While I find your dogs magnificent, I may as well be frank. I am shocked that you drivers are so young. I question whether it would be prudent to trust myself to schoolboys. Nor will I need to interview your man at Porcupine. Fortunately, I have already settled the guide question."

Sandy was listening, open-mouthed, and Beaver was studying the window shade.

"Yes, I have engaged a leader for our expedition, and he will be here by the afternoon train. Now that I find you so inexperienced I shall be glad to have his advice in buying provisions. We will pull up stakes tomorrow, directly after lunch.

"The man I have engaged is a thorough woodsman, from St. Jocelyn, near Quebec. He is a good cook, a remarkable shot, and devoted to our family. Immediately I had your acceptance I telegraphed him. I am fortunate to get such an experienced man for ten dollars a day. But I am a business woman, and quite used to taking decisions."

"Does he speak Eskimo?" blurted out Sandy. "Does he know ice, the spring ice that we must travel over?"

The lady waved her hand petulantly. "He has spent a lifetime in the woods. And doesn't it freeze everywhere in Canada? So of course he knows ice."

"He no spik Eskimo?" Beaver insisted timidly.

The lady was genuinely annoyed. "He knows sign language, just as I do, and he speaks beautiful Quebec French." The subject was closed.

Speechlessness settled deeper upon the partners. They stared at their employer, then at one another. But when the lady excused herself, Sandy cut across to the station, where an obliging telegrapher promised to tell Bumbly Bill that Oscar Birdseed need not wait at the Factory. A guide had been appointed.

Octave was a debonair figure of a man, as he swung down from the train; broad, erect, red lips and cheeks, a black beard nicely parted and brushed to either side. Balanced lightly upon the balls of his feet, cap in hand, he approached Mrs. Armitage and bent low over her glove. He was the picture of the perfect woodsman, the ideal *voyageur des bois*. Sandy and Beaver could not withhold their admiration, even their envy. He had everything. He showed his teeth, white and even as a rodent's, as he shook hands with them. His exclamations over the dogs were appropriate, but Sandy noticed that he missed the key points which made them champions.

The nerve-racking day and evening were at length over. In the stable yard the dogs had burrowed into the snow and were peacefully asleep. The partners, on the straw inside the stable, snuggled into their sleeping bags. They were holding sleep at arm's length, however.

"Bad medicine. She toc-toc," grunted Beaver.

"She's plain bugs, if you ask me," said Sandy dispiritedly. "But it's her money, and her husband. And her life, too, I suppose. But that doesn't mean that we can let Octave and the lady down. We won't do that. We'll

help them run their show the way they want. We'll sell them a good team and a good outfit, at a reasonable price. We can spare the dogs. And we'll find them a good driver, too. And furnish all the dog chow they need. That's the best way out, for us and for them, don't you think?"

"Uh-huh," from the other sack.

The purchases of the following morning were bulky. Octave meant to eat well, and expected to be gone a long time. With the considerable cargo already entrusted to it, the ten-foot komatik could only accommodate two passengers. Sandy would stand on the projecting runners. Beaver and Octave would run alongside, turn and turn about. With a low bow, the guide propped his duffle bag at the rear of the load, making a backrest for Mrs. Armitage, and fixed a seat for himself at the front.

At the end of five miles Sandy tapped the guide on the shoulder with the butt of his whip.

"Your turn to run. Beaver's turn to ride."

Octave indignantly raised on his elbow.

"Me, run? I gallop like a dog? Me, I carry hundred-twenty pound on back, walk all day. But run like dog, ne-vaire."

In that brief exclamation did Octave proclaim himself a man of the forest trail and the canoe, but not a man of the ice and dog team. And in those moments, while Octave asserted his authority and his employer beamed approval, the indecision of the partners hardened into a flat determination. Upon no terms would they be members of the lady's expedition.

It was a tense half-hour, four days later, in the Mackays' sitting room, when Sandy, after talking things over with his mother and father, informed Mrs. Armitage that he and Beaver would have to be counted out of her plans. The lady stormed. Her nerves and her tongue ran wild. Sandy would not have believed that a person could use so many words so fast. But he held himself in. He had sense to know that he must stay calm, until the lady had unpacked her bundle of grievances.

"What am I to think of you?" she exclaimed. "First you try to charge me for four days' wages when you are working for others. Now that I am here, at the last gasp of. no-man's land, you do not keep your word. You accepted to go. By any standard of honor, you boys are crooks."

"Neither of us can go with you and Octave," Sandy

answered softly, "because our minds would be fighting your minds all the time. The whole trip would be one long misunderstanding. Octave would blame us for everything that went wrong. But our dogs will work for you, and really, all that you want of us is a first-class team and an experienced driver. We will gladly furnish that. It will come cheaper, too, than the sum you offered me. Beside that, the outfit will belong to you."

The hint that she would achieve an economy appealed to the lady.

"How do you mean, save money? Be definite, please."

"Get a pencil and add it up," prompted Sandy. "You offered us twenty-five dollars a day, you to furnish food for dogs and driver. Well, I will sell you a team of twelve dogs—you can choose them among our bunch of twenty-five, only my first team being held out. As leader you can choose between Itchy-Koula and Nanuk. Also you may have your choice of our two passenger sleds, also harness, and rations for the team for forty days. For the outfit, all in driving order, we will charge you $360. You said that we were pretty young. The driver we offer you, Middle Beaver, is twenty. He speaks some Eskimo, and his wages are four dollars a day.

"If you have made the total, for a trip for forty days," continued Sandy, warming to his subject, "you will see that what I am now proposing, including Middle Beaver's wages, will cost you just one-half of what you offered me. Best of all, at the end, the team will be your own, to sell or give away or keep. Should you drive to Cochrane, you may sell it for almost as much as you paid. Isn't that a fair offer?"

The lady nibbled her pencil, sceptically, and retired to ask John Mackay's advice. A short conversation with the unemotional manager convinced her that the boys' offer was financially advantageous. Moreover, she had no option. If she were sincere in her desire to get to her husband and back to civilization before the break-up of the ice, there was no time for dallying. Octave jumped at the boys' proposal. In fact, had Mrs. Armitage's mind been less harassed, she might have questioned the motive behind her guide's enthusiasm at having an Indian driver rather than Sandy, and at having a team which was their own, without strings.

To pay the boys, Mrs. Armitage asked Mr. Mackay to cash travellers' checks. Upon Octave's suggestion, she took a further step. She changed the whole of her remaining credit into bills of small denomination.

"It is dangerous to carry all that cash upon your person," objected the Factor, with a sober face. "You are entering a raw, lonesome country. The law and its protection is far behind. You will be among famished folk, who would cut your throat for a pound of bacon or a stick of tobacco. They know that you are in their power. It is a grave error, Madame, to expose them to unnecessary temptation."

"But Octave says that we shall need to have our money easily available, in small bills. He says that the natives prefer it in that form, and that it is the custom to pay the driver and guide each week in cash."

The Factor bit his lip. He had never heard of such a custom.

"At least, Madame, you will carry it well concealed and have your revolver loaded."

"Oh, I always carry my valuables in this leather pouch, attached to my waist. And Octave is a capital shot. I am one of the rare women, you know, who think of everything."

The Factor took another bite of his nether lip. Mr. Mackay didn't seem very convinced.

13. *The Green Leaves Man*

NORTH of the white man's country, upon the eastern fringe of Hudson Bay, are four sites where clans of the Eskimo people, time out of mind, have built their winter homes of rock, snow, and ice blocks. Beginning at the south, and working north along the shore, the settlements are U-Ming-Mac, A-Kim-Si-Ki, Us-Tik-A-Ah, and Nitti-Mis-Kim. Beyond, and farthest north, is Cape Dufferin. Instead of setting his course for the southernmost and nearest of these villages, Octave had boldly decided to make his bid for the point farthest north, Cape Dufferin, and from there work south. Four hundred and eighty miles of open, frozen Bay thus separated him from his first port of call. Seasoned Bay men shook their heads dubiously.

"I prefer to get the hardest leg of the trip behind me at once," he announced, somewhat vaingloriously. "I am that sort of man."

On March tenth, with the first light of morning, the sledge of Mrs. Armitage reposed upon the ice opposite the Factory. Octave had packed it expertly and he and his patron were snugly tucked in atop the load. As Middle Beaver whistled and cracked his whip, six pairs of dogs, with Nanuk in the lead, fell into their stride. The little group on the bank, Mr. and Mrs. Mackay, the Beavers, Sandy, and Sally, gave a cheer. The search for the strayed Professor was on the march.

The partners swallowed hard as they saw their dogs, driven and owned by others, disappear in the distance. But it was no use wasting tears in vain regret. This adventure was not for them. And they had twenty-two miles to cover, and ore to load before night. So they shut their teeth, snapped their teams to the toboggans, and set out for the mine. Sally busied herself within the kennel, a trifle down-cast because of the absence of familiar doggy faces. The old treadmill was resumed. Excitement, fickle hussy, had passed them by.

Day would follow day, as though Octave and a lost botanist had never interrupted the routine of short-haul freighters.

Father Antoine was due to arrive at Porcupine on his pre-spring visit, any day now. When he did come, his first word, as the wind hustled him through the door of the Mackays' dwelling, was as to Sandy's whereabouts.

"He will be back with a load of ore this afternoon, and home for supper," answered Mrs. Mackay.

"Good," said the priest. "Will you tell him and John that I want speech with them in private, as soon as convenient."

Supper over, and before the conviviality of the evening should begin, the Factor led the way to his office. Both he and Sandy were impressed by the gravity of the priest's manner.

"I will relate the facts as briefly as I can," he began at once. "A fortnight ago an Eskimo searched me out, saying that he had something and wanted to know whether it had trade value. He handed me a tight wad which turned out to be five one-dollar bills. As their language has no word for paper, he called them green leaves. I replied that it was the white man's best money.

He wanted stemmo for them. I gave him what tobacco I could spare, as well as tea and sugar. He was delighted, and said that now he would give the green-leaves-man whatever he asked.

"Naturally I was curious. The Eskimo hailed from Issi-Kita, south of U-Ming-Mac, where a sub-clan, descendants of the same great-grandmother, sometimes hunts late in the season. My native said that he and his uncle were about forty miles north of their village. It was the opening of winter, no ice in the Bay as yet, but cold. A white man waved his arms and shouted from the shore. He was emaciated, bare-headed, and empty-handed. The soles had been worn from his shoes. Not an intelligible syllable passed between them, but they saw his misery and paddled him to Issi-Kita. The man had a watch and a fine knife which he presented to the headman, who housed him in his hut. The uncooked meat and rancid fat of the Eskimo diet evidently did not agree with the stranger. He had spasms of vomiting, coughing, and shivering. With half an eye they could see that he was not long for this world. All he possessed was a packet of the green leaves, which he distributed generously to whomever was kind to him.

"Tonight the white-haired stranger at Issi-Kita may

be dead," pursued the priest. "It is two weeks since I saw my native, and he then said that the game had moved on, and his sub-clan would return to U-Ming-Mac in a week or ten days. The stranger was too weak

to travel. The clan could not remain to starve. What was there to do, save to leave him in a hut?"

Sandy and his father leaned forward eagerly, certain of what was to come.

"I have recently heard of the Armitage party," continued Father Antoine. "Is this man a member of that scientific expedition? Is he Professor Armitage himself? I believed that Sandy might care to take a gamble on it. With the speed you make, it is but a trifle over two days to Issi-Kita, three at the outside. Oscar Birdseed was in the Company store today. He knows that coast like his pocket. The course is fourteen degrees east of north. Two low hills, just alike, the only elevations anywhere for miles. A small river between the two hills, and Issi-Kita at the mouth of it.

"You might save a life, Sandy, or earn a big reward. Anyway, it's a sporting chance, the kind of trip that might appeal to a keen boy like you. You are making money and can afford to pay Oscar three dollars a day, to be doubled if you bring in the old man. I wanted to tell you at once. If it is Armitage, his wife, on that roundabout course, is bound to be too late. It would be quite a joke on this man Octave if the Professor were only three days from home and if it were you, after all, who rescued him."

Sandy stood before the priest, his eyes shining. "If I can find Oscar and bring him here, will you tell him what you have told me? He will pay more attention to you."

"Certainly I will," said the Padre heartily. "And with him I'll emphasize the reward part of it."

Birdseed, at his brother's cabin, was lying on his blankets, gazing into the fire, when Sandy knocked. He was a morose man, uncertain of temper, who had worked hard all his life and had nothing to show for it.

"The Pere Antoine is at our house," said Sandy, "and has something to tell you. It's very important."

"No go tonight," mumbled the half-breed. "Sleep now."

"There will be a lot of money, a reward," persisted Sandy.

The trapper studied the flames, then reached for his mukluks.

"If you fooling, I skin your hide."

The priest was persuasive, but Oscar's first verdict was "No go. Too tired." But what had he to lose, urged the priest, except four or five days' time, for which he would be getting three dollars a day and fed. The sled would be light; he could ride like a king in his chariot.

"We think that the man is a big scholar back in the States," added Sandy. "If we save his life, he ought to reward us well. Whatever he gives me, I will divide in three parts; one for you, one for me, one for the team."

The argument that eventually overcame the half-breed's inertia was the thought that he would be outwitting Octave. It had rankled that, after being half-promised the place as Mrs. Armitage's guide, the prize had been snatched away. He nursed a grudge against the man who, he felt, had robbed him of a nice job. It would be sweet as honey to step in and steal the Professor from under Octave's nose.

"O.K. I go," he yielded at last. "But we go quick."

"As soon as I can get the stuff together in the morning," promised Sandy.

The priest repeated his directions. Though there seemed no sign of life, they should examine the interior of every hut. The American would be feeble, perhaps unconscious. They must carry the spirit stove, cocoa, canned milk and soup, ointment and bandages for frostbite, blankets and thick clothing.

"My chief anxiety," resumed the Father, "is that the natives will have left some days ago, and he will have lacked vitality to hold out. The wolves are daring, now, at the end of winter, but I question whether they would venture through the tunnel into a house."

The trip was run off like a machine, swiftly, efficiently, and silently. The dogs were glad not to be hauling a ton of rock, and put all they had into the run. In two days, Oscar spoke two words.

At last the silhouette of the two hills, with the intervening valley, was cut against the glow of the polar lights. The stars were vivid and near, the air biting. From a distance of several miles the dogs had scented human habitations, and had revived with the thought of food and a night's rest. The eight tupeks—permanent huts of stone, twelve to sixteen feet in diameter—which bore the name of Issi-Kita, were erected without plan upon a rocky field, and were no more than mounds on the surface of the snow. Footprints led everywhere, connecting the huts and along the stream. But there was no barking of dogs, no answer to the halloos of the newcomers. Sandy parked the sledge at the entrance of what seemed the principal tupek, and stretched his tie line.

"We don't dare wait until morning. Here is my torch, Oscar. Go through the houses while I feed the team."

But instead of examining the huts, the half-breed first went to the shore, and out upon the ice.

"Fifteen big, ten little. Powder blow in track. He gone three-four day," was his diagnosis of the size and whereabouts of the population of Issi-Kita.

"They will have left food for the white man. Maybe

he is living. Go quick into the houses. Begin with this one. Hurry, hurry," commanded the boy, flinging out chucks of frozen fish. He fed until the dogs asked for no more. At that instant Oscar shouted.

During the ensuing weeks, Dr. Armitage was many times asked to recount his sensations when first he heard Oscar's voice, saw the beam of light, and realized that he was by way of being given a fresh lease on life. He had been in a stupor. Fibers of dried meat, that he had been trying to chew, dangled from the corner of his mouth. Too weak to rise, he had strength to prop himself upon his elbow, among the heap of caribou hides. His lips moved, but only husky rattles came out.

"My first consciousness," related the Doctor afterward, "was the barking of dogs. I supposed them to be wolves. Wolves had sniffed around the walls on previous nights, and I thought they had returned. But I did not fear them, for the natives, before leaving, had piled the tunnel with stones. Then I heard a voice speaking English. Hands were pulling away the stones. A torch dazzled my eyes. I must have fainted.

"The next I knew the blue light of a spirit lamp was burning under a pan, from which rose the steam of beef broth. Two men were in the hut with me. Mittens were on my swollen hands. Instead of the scraps of skin I had bound about my head, I was wearing a fur cap. Around my body and limbs were blankets. They were holding hot tea, with a dash of brandy, to my lips."

The Professor was imperious upon one point. "I cannot permit criticism of the Eskimo clan at Issi-Kita for abandoning me. It was in harmony with their tribal custom. It was not in their power to bring me back to vigor. They would have done precisely the same thing with a decrepit or dying member of their own family. My vitality had been steadily diminishing. We all knew that my time had come. What was written, was written.

"Among the Eskimos, as among the animals, the Indians, and all primitive peoples, the expiring member goes quietly apart and lets nature take its course. There is resignation, but no fear of the end. I was more than half dead when Sandy and Oscar arrived. In another forty-eight hours I would have been beyond human aid. And I know that I should have gone the remainder of my journey toward death without pain of body or rebellion of spirit. I realize, as I hadn't before, that the treatment which Eskimos and Indians accord their aged and their incurably ill, has a deep philosophy of mercy to recommend it. The Great Spirit comes for his child without human interference."

At the end of three days, although the Professor was still unable to wait on himself, the tide of health had turned. He was lucid. He relished his food. And it was he himself who insisted that the return journey not be delayed. They drove by easy stages, hugging the coast, that more protected sites might be chosen for camp. Sandy handled his team, and Oscar gave undivided attention to the invalid.

To Sandy's astonishment the taciturn trapper turned out to be a natural nurse. The touching dependence of the elderly scientist upon him seemed to have wakened something new in the half-breed's character. Nor did this relationship of patient and nurse end with the party's arrival at Porcupine. Oscar borrowed a mattress of Mother Swain and installed the Professor in his brother's cabin. It would have been more suitable, perhaps, had the convalescent gone to the Swains or the Mackays. But the Professor could have all of Oscar's time, as cook, valet, and nurse, and also he could pay Oscar and not feel that he was trespassing. Every two hours the invalid had his light nourishment. To supplement the canned butter, milk and meat from the Com-

pany store, Oscar would slip off into the bush with his
shotgun. A stew of hare, or snowy bunting, or lem-
ming, or a broiled ptarmigan would vary the menu of
chef Oscar.

Fact by fact, as they travelled home, and subsequently, in the Birdseed cabin,
the Professor volunteered high-
lights of his wanderings. Sandy
and Oscar had agreed between
themselves not to question him.
In his own way, at his own time,
he would tell them what he
wanted to tell. While at Issi-Kita
his mind had been too full of
horror. They respected his ret-

icence, and even went further. Until he should be stronger and master of his nerves, they conspired not to tell him of the expedition of Mrs. Armitage and Octave. The Mackays and persons to whom he might talk were pledged to the same silence. The scientist had already been subjected to enough worries.

The Professor's scientific party had gotten off on the wrong foot, due to the dishonesty of their head guide, who turned out to be a thorough rascal and decamped with the maps, money, a rifle and a canoe. After that it seemed to have been uneventful and reasonably successful from a botanical standpoint, until a blizzard caught them unprepared. They had overstayed their season. They were two scientists and two guides, on the upper waters of Big River. Their canoes and most of their supplies were lost in the three-day storm. In desperate straits, they built two rafts, although the wood was green and small. One scientist and one guide embarked upon each raft. In company, the rafts floated toward the Bay, until, during a prolonged fog, they lost touch with one another. The Professor and his guide still had a rifle, ammunition, and an axe, and a handful of flour and tea. They reached the margin of Hudson Bay without further mishap. Here they hung about for several days without discovering any trace of their colleagues.

The two men then started south on foot. At this point there was a dispute, the guide wishing to travel north, believing in this direction they would stand a better chance of encountering native settlements. The Professor's feet went back on him, and their progress was painful and slow. Weather grew daily more severe. One afternoon they made camp early. The guide went inland to cut firewood. In the hope of potting something for supper he took the rifle also. The Professor never saw him again. Whether the man wilfully deserted his employer or whether he came to grief, might never be known.

Once convinced that he was alone, the Professor buried the tin box containing his diary and his botanical data, under a protruding white rock, on a promontory, a hundred feet in from the waterfront, and about two hundred and fifty miles north of Issi-Kita. At times the old man wandered along the beach, at times inland, looking for berries. He must have passed U-Ming-Mac on one of these inland excursions, without knowing it. Each step gave torturing pain. Occasionally he found a fish that had been washed ashore. Once he killed a porcupine with a club and ate it raw. His main sustenance was the berries, frozen upon the bush, the crowberry, the whortleberry and the bear berry. As food grew scarcer, the scientist thought of nothing else, and devoted most of his remaining strength to an endless search for something—anything—to eat.

Forty miles north of Issi-Kita two hunters in kayaks came ashore. They saw his bleeding feet and understood. Each man was in a decked-over skin canoe, barely large enough for himself. In addition, the interior of the canoe was loaded with meat which they were taking home. They lashed the two light craft, side by side, and the Professor lay crossways upon the two decks, behind the backs of the paddlers. They were able to accomplish this extraordinary feat of seamanship because the prevailing wind over the Bay is easterly, and with the off-shore breeze the sea was calm. But during the forty-mile trip the Professor said that his head and feet were never more than two inches above the water.

"They did what they could for me," testified Dr. Armitage with appreciation. "What they ate was awful, but they gave me the same as they fed their own children. All I had to offer in exchange was a watch, a clasp knife, a handful of safety-pins and a packet of greenbacks. You may be sure that I was glad to give them."

At Porcupine Dr. Armitage picked up strength daily, sitting before the cabin, eating Oscar's spider-bread—soda biscuit cooked in bacon fat in a frying pan—and sinking his teeth in a caribou or moose steak as often as Chief Beaver or Oscar killed meat for the hungry man.

His first promenade was on a still Sunday afternoon when the partners were not hauling ore. Leaning on Oscar's arm, he came to inspect the shop and the kennel, and to renew acquaintance with the white team that had ferried him back to civilization.

During the four weeks since his return, the Professor had not once mentioned money, either as wages during the rescue trip, or as payment for Oscar's care and food. Beaver, Sandy and Oscar had agreed that they would let the first word on the subject come from the scientist.

At the close of his afternoon call, he pulled a paper from his pocket.

"I want you good friends to read the copy of a telegram I sent yesterday. Read it aloud, Sandy."

Prairie State Trust Company, Chicago.

Kindly transmit the sum of five hundred American dollars to Royal Bank of Cochrane for credit of Sandy Mackay stop also same amount to same bank for credit of Oscar Birdseed stop these amounts in currency to be shipped to Hudson's Bay Company Factory Porcupine at the reopening of rail traffic.

Rigby Armitage

"As you know, my pockets are empty, and this is the best I can do," explained the Doctor. "Everything is turning out nicely, except that I am distressed by the silence of my wife. I have wired her twice, without reply. I must hurry home on her account. Perhaps Sandy or Beaver will drive me to Cochrane. We'll set a date before next Sunday."

The partners and Oscar exchanged glances. As the Professor took a few steps before the door, Oscar whispered, "Him gotta know quick."

But before another Sunday could roll around, the Professor was travelling north as fast as Quicksilver and eighteen dogs, their bellies to the ice, could carry him.

14. Octave's True Colors

ACROSS the icy Bay, the Armitage-Octave expedition encountered intolerable weather. Facing the pelting wind, the eyes of the dogs froze shut. Frequent stops were necessary to let the animals bite out the caked powder from between their toes. Among the serrated valleys and crags of snow, the top-heavy sledge was an abominable nuisance.

Ponderous masses of ice formed sculptured ridges, like up-ended geological strata. Under enormous pressure from below and from the sides, the frozen surface of the Bay bulged and buckled, shattered and erupted, with the report of artillery. There was no sound but the fury of the wind and the ice, no color save the ghostly pallor which was no color at all. Mrs. Armitage was obliged to make the detours on foot, while Middle Beaver and Octave, one on either side, prevented the sledge from capsizing.

Octave was hopelessly misled by his compass. The magnetic pole, which controls the needle of the compass, was no longer to the north, but to the east. He set the course too far north, then too far to the east. Finally he could do no better than observe a general north-easterly direction, which he checked by an occasional glimpse of the sun or of some familiar star.

Middle Beaver and Octave now added to the general unhappiness by a series of quarrels. In the hit-or-miss, unsystematic fashion of the Indian, the driver fed his dogs more than the allotted daily ration. When an Indian has provisions he uses them, with little forethought for next week. That is what provisions are for. It will be time to worry when next week comes. The team was having a heavy drag of it, and the driver wanted to keep stout hearts in them.

The expedition had left Porcupine with forty days' rations of fish and corn meal for the team. But it required nineteen days, instead of the anticipated ten, to sight Cape Dufferin. And due to the driver's lavish feeding, only ten days' dog rations remained. Octave flew into a passion with Middle Beaver, who thereupon went to the opposite extreme, and let the animals go to bed half-fed. As a result they lost their snap and speed, and grew quarrelsome among themselves.

A fox crossed the trail one day, in plain sight. The underfed beasts ran wild, upsetting the sledge, giving Mrs. Armitage a nasty spill, and leaving Octave five miles in the rear. Middle Beaver was now blamed for his poor control of the team.

But most serious was the dispute between Octave and the Indian over money. At Cape Dufferin it came to a head, although it had been smouldering since the first pay day. The guide had requested that they be paid weekly in cash. He now insisted that, as head of the party, he was entitled to a commission on the wages of those under him. He said it was the established rule among guides. In short, he demanded that Middle Beaver contribute a daily dollar to him. The driver refused. On the third pay day, as Octave threatened violence, Beaver took his story to Mrs. Armitage. She sided with the Indian. But Octave persisted that the dollar a day was legally his, and that if Beaver did not pay it, Mrs. Armitage must. If she refused, he would not move another step. It was a bare-faced hold-up, but from that day the guide's wage was eleven dollars a day.

At Dufferin they found Eskimo huts, but the inhabitants were elsewhere, as this folk wander over a wide area in search of food. No sign of Professor Armitage or his scientific party was found, and the rescuers turned south.

Octave wasted two days' food in the hope of shooting a polar bear. The white bear, who does not sleep during the winter, exists on what he gets from the seal holes. The seal weighs a hundred pounds, the bear can eat sixty pounds. After each repast of the bear, therefore, forty pounds are left for the wolves. The stages of this drama can be read in the bloody snow tracks where the seals come up to breathe. Octave, who enjoyed his food, conceived the idea of securing fresh meat. He crouched within range of a likely hole for two days, but the bear was wary. The guide could shoot seal at will, but, as he had no harpoon to land them, they dropped into the depths like so many stones.

A suspicion was taking root in Mrs. Armitage's mind. Was Octave deliberately prolonging the trip into the longest possible number of pay days? He was receiving exceptional wages, and Middle Beaver was doing the hard work. This first suspicion was soon reinforced by a second, and one more sinister. She came to believe that Octave neither wished nor intended to find her husband. From a study of the chart—a study, unfortunately, undertaken too late to help the situation—she was convinced that her husband could never have reached a point so far north as Cape Dufferin. The costly and nerve-searing trip across the ice from Porcupine had been no more than a piece of grandiose bluff on the man's part.

There was certainly something underhanded in the guide's connection with the scientific party. When questioned, he answered evasively. With a shock, she recollected that, since he left Lindsay Inlet, she knew nothing of her husband save what Octave himself had told her. He had been her husband's chief guide in Labrador. His story was plausible. He said that he had cut his foot with an axe and had returned home, in order that he might not retard the party's progress. But how much of this, if any, was true?

The shortage of fuel was another hardship. North of the timber line the natives burn moss or peat, which their women folk collect and dry during the summer.

Mrs. Armitage's expedition was using a single-burner spirit stove. As the tins of alcohol grew few she lighted it but seven minutes each day, only long enough to melt snow and boil water for tea.

It was, therefore, a mutually antagonistic, mutually suspicious trio of rescuers who drove into Nitti-Mis-Kim. No word of the scientists was obtainable. These natives, however, had an abundance of meat. They had killed a walrus and a white whale. The white whale goes south in winter, but occasionally a late-stayer will become impounded in an inner pond of ice-bound water, where he remains until he suffocates, or is harpooned by the Eskimos.

Middle Beaver, acting as interpreter, bartered tea, sugar and tobacco for the sorely needed dog meat. After a two-day rest, despite Octave's reluctance, Mrs. Armitage insisted upon resuming the journey. The guide claimed that drinking snowwater had given him the colic, and that, after the privations to which he had been subjected, he rated a week's repose. He was still grumbling when he took his seat upon the sledge.

They reached Us-Tik-A-Ah at nightfall of the fifteenth day from Cape Dufferin, and the thirty-fourth day from Porcupine. Dog rations had been exhausted two days before. Paper money was unknown to the natives and was refused. As they had no food to exchange, Mrs. Armitage traded her watch for two seals.

They had come to the upper margin of the timber region, and the waist-high, lichen-encrusted white spruce furnished them the pleasures of a fire. They celebrated with a stew of seal meat. Mrs. Armitage made a wry face, but swallowed a few morsels. Octave said that he was not accustomed to such food, and dined upon a can of beef-hash which he had secreted in his bed roll. Middle Beaver licked the pot clean. He was right at home with seal stew.

At Us-Tik-A-Ah, as elsewhere, no trace was found of Professor Armitage. But the size and strength of the dogs excited envy. It was absolutely necessary to obtain sufficient dog meat to get to the next village. The headman would furnish seal in exchange for four dogs. Nothing else that Mrs. Armitage possessed was of interest to him. With two swings gone, Nanuk and four couples remained.

"Fewer to feed. Load little now," philosophized Middle Beaver.

But during the early morning hours, almost at the moment they were to set out for A-Kim-Si-Ki, Nanuk ran head foremost into a booby trap, set by a pack of white wolves, and lost his life. It was a trick as old as Adam. A yearling pup, let alone a lead dog, should not have been so stupid. Middle Beaver was also partly to blame for not chaining his leader more carefully.

A single wolf slunk among the huts. Barking valiantly, Nanuk, who had worked out of his collar, gave chase. Out upon the Bay fled the seemingly terrified intruder, with Nanuk in hot and noisy pursuit. Then the six wolves, who had been lying prone upon the snow, three on a side, closed in behind. Nanuk's loss was a crippling blow. Now only four swings remained, and, leaderless, Middle Beaver himself would be obliged to run at the head of his team. Octave, to his disgust, would have to walk.

At A-Kim-Si-Ki, six days later, the condition of the ice gave occasion for a fresh anxiety. Progress had been slow. Man and animal were underfed and overstrained. The human beings were eating the corn meal porridge which had been intended for the dogs. It was the nineteenth of April, and a thaw was due. A rising temperature would disengage the ice from the shore.

Middle Beaver, in his imperfect English, tried to explain to his employer what happened every spring.

Far out in the Bay, a storm would make waves, which in turn would crumple the weakened surface of the ice. Once the initial rupture was made, floating islands would sliver off, and, propelled by the wind, drift outward. The great islands would divide into smaller islands. Channels of open water would baffle travellers, who must make exploratory detours, and perhaps retrace their steps for miles. In the maze of waterways, there would finally be no means of reaching the shore. Being blown into Hudson Bay on a melting cake of ice is a fate which the hardiest dreads to think upon.

At A-Kim-Si-Ki, Octave delivered an ultimatum. He was chief guide, responsible for the well-being of the party. As such he commanded that the search for the Professor be abandoned. They must wait where they were until the ice went out. Later they could return to Porcupine by canoe.

"But what shall we live upon? It will be six weeks at least," wailed Mrs. Armitage, her nerve failing. "We have nothing left to trade, and nothing to eat."

"I have thought of all that," drawled the guide, with an insolence that he had lately affected. "You still have eight dogs and a sledge, several handsome bracelets, a revolver and a knife, four pairs of extra blankets, a fur coat that you are not wearing, and quite a number of those five-dollar bills. Perhaps these natives, who are nearer trading posts, will accept the white man's money. When the ice moves out we can net whitefish, which are delicious. While we wait we shall be well fed and comfortable here at A-Kim-Si-Ki."

"And do you expect me to pay you eleven dollars a day," stammered the lady, aghast, "while you oblige us to waste time here?"

"Certainly, Madame, we are still on the expedition, are we not?" His smirk had malice.

Mrs. Armitage lost her temper, from top to bottom.

"You are no more than a small-time, oily tongued grafter. More than that, it is my belief that you never intended finding my husband. I don't know your secret, but you don't dare meet him, face to face. You are a rascal and a coward. And probably a lot of worse things."

Still pale with rage, Mrs. Armitage went to find Middle Beaver. The Indian believed that if they travelled early and late—for daylight was growing longer—stayed close to the land, and watched the movement of the ice scrupulously, they could get to U-Ming-Mac, and from thence, perhaps, to Rupert's House. It was in these localities that traces of the Professor would most probably be found. But the ice would not wait.

Mrs. Armitage acted within the hour. She bartered her revolver, her fur coat, her jewelry, and two more dogs, with the clansmen, for smoked caribou meat and seal. She and Middle Beaver still had six dogs and an almost empty sledge. They were on the point of departure when Octave swaggered past, and blocked the trail.

"And my wages, Madame? As you will not be here on pay days, I must ask you to settle in advance."

She stood up to him squarely.

"Not one cent, you contemptible robber."

The guide shifted the rifle from the bend of his arm, pointing it at the head of the first dog.

"If you do not pay me six weeks in advance, I will shoot every dog you have. And I give you five minutes to put the money in my hand."

She capitulated. Middle Beaver did not comprehend the details of their conversation, but he did plainly see Octave block their path, aim a gun at Mrs. Armitage, who was unarmed, and not lower his rifle until she had counted a stack of bills into his hand. And it is of interest to note that these facts, when the Indian gave his testimony, three months later, before the magistrate, were of conclusive importance.

The komatik now carried only the bare essentials. With Octave left behind, they travelled faster and breathed easier. Middle Beaver had but a half-team, but he had the lungs and the piano-wire flanks that carried him all day at a fast, choppy trot. He was cautious, and climbed a promontory or ridge, to examine the further ice, before deciding upon the next half-day's run. He tied a strap at the head of the trunk line to which the dogs were hitched, looped it around his shoulder, and not only guided the team but pulled with it.

Night and morning he studied the horizon. It was nearing the end of April, and the dreaded thaw and break-up of winter could not be much longer delayed. In his eagerness to make distance the boy allowed himself no more than a five-hours' rest at night.

They were running a daily marathon, in competition with the elements. Six lean and foot-sore dogs and an over-driven young Indian, who felt that the honor of his race rested upon his shoulders, were pitted against the Unknown. From now forward each additional half-day of calm, which permitted a few further homeward miles, was the special gift of Heaven.

U-Ming-Mac lies upon a point. To the north of the cur-infested hamlet is a bay, twelve miles across and indenting the coast to a depth of thirty miles. To insure safety and stick to the shore line, as Middle Beaver had heretofore been doing, would mean a run of sixty miles. But before deciding upon the cross-country route, Middle Beaver waited for full daylight. He mounted the highest ledge of the shore and peered long and carefully at the twelve blue-grey miles. Faintly he could discern the dots that were the Eskimo settlement. But what he was searching for were streaks of a darker blue, patterns in black, for these would be open water. He could detect none.

"Guess today him good," he reported to Mrs. Armitage, who was resting on the sled. "We go."

Out from the shelter of the land the wind was brisk. It drew down the thirty miles of the bay, as through a stovepipe. The Indian scowled at the sudden freshening of the air. His features were set. Leaning forward against his shoulder strap, he was trotting smoothly and fast, his step timed to two steps of the dogs. So far as he could judge he had come more than halfway across the inlet.

It was Mrs. Armitage who screamed.

"Look, Beaver! The whole bay is moving! We are cut off, in front and behind."

Its ties to the land weakened by the milder temperature of April, and urged outward by the lively offshore breeze, the ice upon the western end of the estuary had broken free of its bonds. With majestic deliberation the vast surface was sailing seaward. Already a quarter-mile of blue water separated it from its parents.

There was still a single point of contact between the vagabond island and solid land. On the U-Ming-Mac side, the edge of the moving block was bumping and scraping against the shore ice. Until the innermost corner of the island should have drifted beyond the stationary ice, it would be possible to leap across the gap. Instantly Middle Beaver sensed his sole chance of escape, and changed his direction.

"Get odder ice ... before he goes," he panted, calling to his dogs to make the final sprint with him.

Four miles were still to go. It was heart-breaking, their display of courage and will. Heart-breaking, because they were bound to lose. Middle Beaver measured the distance with his eye and knew that the seaward-sailing floe would have passed a point of contact before he could make it. He and his dogs were running their hearts out, but they were not quite good enough.

His last despairing hope, as he whipped himself forward, was that sharp eyes at U-Ming-Mac might have seen them, and would launch kayaks or canoes.

★ ★ ★

Sandy and Oscar had borrowed the Professor's marine glasses and climbed the hog-back to the east of the village. They wanted to study the inlet before attempting a crossing. The party in pursuit of Mrs. Armitage, which her husband had organized the instant he learned that she had been hoodwinked by his own renegade guide, and was even then at the man's mercy somewhere among the Eskimo clans, was four days out from Porcupine. They had made camp at U-Ming-Mac the previous nightfall.

Oscar pointed. "Small hitch come across. Six dog."

"Let me have a squint." But Sandy's young eyes needed no glasses. Yanking Oscar's sleeve, he broke into a run, shouting as he went.

"It's Middle Beaver. Six of our dogs. One person on the sled. See the break, half up the bay? They are drifting out. Snap in the dogs. Make it fast, Oscar, fast!"

The Professor tumbled upon the sled while they rushed the dogs to their stations. The sky had cleared, the ice shone brilliantly blue and brittle. At the point where the seaward-drifting floe was grating its edge along the shore field, the gap was a foot wide. Dogs and sled took the space in their stride. Looking anxiously eastward Sandy's eye measured the few hundred yards that remained to pass before the island would forever lose contact with the shore.

When dog teams meet, particularly teams which know one another, first one dog, then another, lifts his muzzle in a full-throated howl. This salute now began. But Middle Beaver, plowing forward in a straight line, did not slacken. He pointed to the two edges in contact, their single avenue of escape. Sandy pointed to the same spot. Not a word was spoken. Every second counted now. In a wide curve, barely slackening speed, Quicksilver veered his heavy team, until they had swung into a course parallel with Middle Beaver's and were closing up the opening.

As he breezed past, Sandy leaned outward, grasped the strap looped over Middle Beaver's shoulder, and wrapped it around the upright of his own komatik.

"Jump on your sled as it goes by," he called to the Indian.

Nineteen fresh dogs were now towing the six tired ones and the sledge of Mrs. Armitage. The tempo of every galloping foot quickened. The final heat of the race for life was on.

Stimulus is infectious. Without knowing just what, each dog on the floating island sensed that something stupendous was hanging by a hair. They ran better than they knew how to run. And always ahead, on his

long free line, danced Quicksilver, his eye upon the corner of the moving floe, his high piercing bark seeming to say, "Come on, girls and boys! Lean on it! A little more speed!"

They came soaring down to the corner. The last rim of the island was now three feet from the shore ice. Each second the opening widened. The momentum of the double team was tremendous. The passengers forgot to breathe. Quicksilver timed his leap beautifully, and his eighteen dogs followed like an undulant wave

of fur. The unusual length of the new komatik, coupled with the momentum, bridged the canal of water.

But the second team came to grief. Being behind, these dogs had not seen the approaching gap. They jerked backward in alarm, and broke the tow strap. The first two pairs landed safely, but the third swing was struggling in the water. The front of the sledge was also in the water, with the rear end still on the floe.

Oscar and Sandy hauled the dripping dogs out by their harness and held the forepart of the sledge against the ice, for Mrs. Armitage and Middle Beaver to clamber off. The island had by now floated beyond the projecting rear runners, and the komatik was sinking. It would have drawn down the dogs attached to it had Middle Beaver not promptly cut the extension line. They all stood on the edge of the shore ice and watched Johnny Dolan's second-hand sled settle from sight. Its work was done.

The Professor folded his long arms around his wife, who, the danger escaped, was crying with happiness. Side by side the couple, and their three friends, stood fascinated. Yard by yard, the island of ice upon which they had so lately been travelling, drifted outward on its pilgrimage of self-destruction.

Mrs. Armitage linked her arm affectionately through that of her husband.

"Did I rescue you, or did you rescue me, or did the Hudson Bay Express save us both?" she asked.

"The ice was bad enough," rejoined the man, "but what I'm chiefly grateful for, is that both of us are out of the hands of Octave."

★ ★ ★

Instructed by Corporal Don, the Professor and his wife drew up an itemized statement of the guide's misdemeanors, which they left at the court house in Cochrane, a month later, when the first train of the season carried them out. In due time Octave was arrested, minus his handsome beard, was made to refund what he had gained through trickery and violence, and was locked up long enough to reflect that an unbridled love of money is indeed a dangerous thing.

At the depot, after they had bought their tickets in Bumbly Bill's freight-car, Doctor and Mrs. Armitage held an impromptu reception. The Professor, from the platform of the car, made a short speech. He said that he looked forward to having a cabin of his own, among the spruce on the banks of the beautiful Abitibi, where he and his wife could spend their summers.

"I'd like to do my annual hunting and fishing, from now on, with Oscar," said the Doctor.

"And I'd like to do mine with Middle Beaver," added his wife.

"We've been through some bad times and a lot of good times together," he concluded. "And this lady and I feel that about the truest friends we have in the world live right here in Porcupine."

People were still clapping when Old Cannonball wheezed out of the yard toward Cochrane.

15. Trials and Troubles

NOTHING had roused the public's imagination more than the plot to bomb the Great Lake cities from the north, and to establish a refuelling station at Sable Island. It had both warned them of an unprotected frontier, and had demonstrated the effective role that the native dog could play in guarding that icebound entry into the heart of Canadian and American manufacturers. They grew suddenly proud of the fuzzy-faced freighter of the snow trails, native son of Greenland, of Labrador, and of the Outer Mackenzie.

The Corporal let it be known that he would keep open house, from eight to eight-thirty each evening, when the dog news was broadcast. He did not intend to be a hoarder with the only receiving set in the village. As many as eleven people sometimes sat on his floor, listening to the spluttering voice of his four-lamp box.

The radio's reference to dogs touched a sympathetic chord throughout the nation. Everyone loves dogs. Everyone, at some period of his life, has had a closer-than-a-brother dog pal. And at a time when all classes of the population were volunteering in an all-out program of defense, why should the wolf-dog—original citizen of Canada—and the man of Indian blood, be overlooked? They could and would cooperate in keeping their wide white areas free.

Secretaries of the Associated Dog Clubs of Canada, convened in a special meeting, proposed a scheme for a string of listening outposts, extending from Ungava Bay to Point Barrow. It was a rational plan, and met with instant public approval. These proposed huts, with inter-post radio communication, spaced at intervals of two hundred miles, were to be connected by cross-country dog routes. With these keen eyes and ears, scientific, human, and animal, on the alert, the probability of enemy landing-fields or fuelling stations being established would be much reduced.

For this frontier patrol service the advantage of dogs was unquestionable. They could penetrate remote ice pockets. They could endure unholy weather. They were cheap. They were already in existence, and only needed to be organized. They were a home-soil product, "made in Canada." In comparison with air travel they required neither repair shops nor mechanics, nor reserves of oil and gasoline. In doing its job the dog-team was silent. It had no motor exhaust to announce its position. More than that, it was easy to conceal, particularly if the dogs were Eskimos of the smoke-grey variety. Taking advantage of the three-minute warning that a cruising plane gives, and with a few yards of sheeting, driver, sled and team could be neatly camouflaged.

As the Dog Clubs sketched out their ocean-to-ocean service, they foresaw three districts: the Atlantic, the Mid-Continent, and the Pacific Zones. For the Atlantic third of the organization, as a beginning, six teams and six drivers would be required. The dogs, harness and sledges were to be bought outright by the government, and the drivers would be under the orders of the regional intelligence officers. The Clubs knew that if their plan worked out successfully, and if the war continued, the army would be ready to take them over.

But the choice of suitable teams was the crux of the problem. The men who had the dog patrol at heart were hard-headed chaps, and soon recognized the difficulties of a too-ardent public sentiment. To weed out fanciers, inexperienced breeders of unsuitable races, and well-meaning amateurs, they announced a National Work Dog Race. Any aspirant with a ten-dog hitch, a sledge and a driver could enter. The cash prize was to be one hundred dollars, but looming behind this cash payment, as an infinitely more potent incentive, was the prestige it would bring to the winner, and the probability that he would be asked to furnish teams for the service.

To remove the competition from political or social influence, the Associated Clubs sent out to Nome for Alonzo Brainard, chairman of the Race Committee of the Cape Nome Dog Club, and authorized him to handle all details of the event.

The clubs could not have made a wiser choice. Mr. Brainard was a two-fisted miner, just past middle-age, of independent fortune, tactful yet outspoken, and a life-long admirer of the husky. He said that he owed his life to a nameless old Malemute mongrel, who had guided him through a blizzard to a settler's cabin, and that he was spending the rest of his days in a sincere effort to pay her back.

Mr. Brainard, after naming the starting date as February 16th, when trail conditions should be at their best, set out to select the route. The Nome Race was over a course of four hundred straight-away miles. But as the patrolling for which these Scout dogs were destined would be over a variety of terrain, he wanted to find a variegated four-day course that would begin and end at North Bay. It should include glare ice upon a body of water, in-and-out dodging through a forest, the crossing of a bald, highland shoulder, where the crust would be slippery, and a zig-zag line among rocks or hillocks.

The judge spent more than a week deciding upon the course. The total circuit, from the North Bay City Hall back again to the City Hall, was four hundred and eighteen miles. Out through the suburbs it capered up-and-down across Excelsior County to Dog Rib. Thence along the slippery Lac des Douze to Anvil. His designated route then bent westward, over the sky-parlor promontory of Adam's Apple, to Brisket. Thereafter, for its fourth leg, it made a southerly curve, through Snidders, Parker's Chapel, and into the outskirts of North Bay. Mr. Brainard felt that he had succeeded well. He had included every type of travel that scouts would be called upon to negotiate.

His two rules could hardly be misunderstood. (1) All dogs that started were to be described in writing by a member of the committee; they were to be checked at the start, at two points during the race, and at the finish line; the same dogs, either running or carried upon the sled, were to be present at the finish as at the start. (2) During the actual running of the race, neither dogs nor drivers should receive outside help, nor be subject to outside interference.

In the hotels and clubs of Canadian cities it was rumored that several big betting rings, composed of wealthy gamblers, were preparing to move to North Bay, and that considerable amounts of money would change hands on the race. This was unfortunate, since, when money was at stake, influence might be brought to bear upon drivers, or tricks played upon the teams. But this was a side of the patriotic sport that neither Mr. Brainard nor the Associated Clubs could control, much as they regretted it.

★ ★ ★

It was the fourth year that Little Beaver and Sandy had been breeding dogs. They were both seventeen. Neither was tall, but both were compact, supple, and muscular, with extraordinary eyesight and hearing. They were harder and more able-bodied than they had ever been. By any standard, they did a big day's work, and did it, moreover, without effort.

It seemed very long ago that they had taken up dog freighting. Then they had been inflamed by romantic ideas of heroic rescues, of hair-trigger escapes from racketeers and spies. But now, at seventeen, they looked back upon these boyish illusions with a tolerant smile. Now they were business men. They had participated in five or six story-book adventures, it is true, but now they were content to settle into the daily duties of sober men-of-affairs.

They had learned to appreciate a crackling fire in the chimney of an evening, sleep in a bed with springs, hot food without wet wood-smoke in their eyes, and dry stockings during the day's tramp. The lure of hardship for hardship's sake had worn thin. After rude trial, they knew that they could run with the dogs against a fifty-mile gale, pass the night in the open, inside layers of fur and felt, with the temperature at fifty below zero, plod forward on empty stomachs for forty-eight hours. They could do these things, certainly, if it were necessary, but they were not keen about it.

Their third season's work for the Three Brothers Mine was going well—the trustworthy sort of business that puts the pay envelope in the workman's pocket every Saturday night. They had four working teams, sixty-two full-grown dogs, and half that number of youngsters who were showing promise. During the summer they had built another kennel, with an airy loft of slats, like a corn crib, for storing smoked fish. As drivers, beside themselves, the partners now had Oscar and Middle Beaver, on weekly wages. On Monday, Wednesday and Friday, Little Beaver and Oscar drove two teams to the mine. On the alternate days, Middle Beaver and Sandy made the trip with two other teams. Bumby Bill's Sally, now a buxom young person and a capable dog-handler, was earning a dollar a day as a fixture at the kennel. Chief Beaver showed his advanced age, but he too, had as much work from the boys as he cared to undertake, tanning moosehide and harpooning seal meat. In a word, the dog business had settled into a pleasant and profitable rut, with everyone eating his fill, liking and trusting every other member of the concern. The partners had outgrown their hankering for novelty. They felt responsible for their invested capital, their animals, and their employees. In John Mackay's iron box were fourteen hundred dollars to their credit, and they found it agreeable, week by week, to increase that sum.

This was the state of the boys' affairs when Corporal Donaldson tapped at the Factory kitchen. It was latish on a mid-January evening, and Sandy, leg-weary from his jaunt from the mine, had yawned more than once.

"Beg pardon for disturbing you so near to bedtime," apologized the policeman, stamping the snow from his boots. "But the Captain has been on the wire from headquarters. It's about the Work-Dog Race. He insists that Sandy and Beaver enter a team, and that one of them drive it. You have been listening to this business on the radio. He won't take no for an answer. While the Dog Clubs, and not the army, are organizing the race, all the same the army is much interested.

"I don't often mix in what is not my business," went on the Corporal, somewhat ill-at-ease. "Your first big stroke of luck was when the Old Racer gave you Ne-Nu-Ka. But this Race is your second opportunity, and a bigger one, believe me. If you take it, whether you win or lose, you will have a hand in organizing a service that the country needs and wants.

"But suppose your answer is no. You may think that you can sit back on your hunkers and stick to ore hauling. Not for long. You and Little Beaver will be drafted before long. What will become of this mess of dog-flesh? With you and Beaver gone, your dogs will be stolen, strayed, starved, or just poisoned as a public nuisance. Without you, your teams are just about worthless. If you don't jump into this Work-Dog Race, Sandy, I advise you, as a friend, to begin tapering off your dog business tomorrow morning."

The visitor stopped, staggered by his own outburst.

"Well, goodnight. I'll be stepping down the trail. Don't move, any of you; I can let myself out."

John Mackay sat long in his chair, without a word, regarding the toes of his woolen stockings. Sandy kissed his mother and went to his room. He felt rather than saw the moisture in her eyes, as she murmured, "My little lad is a man now." It seemed to the boy that circumstances bigger than himself had settled the question. The outside world had edged in on Beaver and himself, presenting a work which they might not like, but which they could not sidestep.

As the boy undressed and lay, open-eyed, in bed, a saying of the Old Racer came back to him: "A race depends more upon the man who fixes things in advance than upon the dogs." Sandy had never raced dogs. Never even witnessed a dog race. But whether he wanted it or not, he felt that he was in this up to his neck. And he would spare neither time nor money to help his animals make a good showing.

He would put himself in the place of the poorest dog, unable to talk, unable to keep up with his faster team-mates, his feet sore, fighting blindly to stick to the heels of the dog in front, to hold the right direction where no foot-prints existed, his stomach empty, during an endless hundred-mile grind. What would he, Sandy Mackay, want, if he were in that weakest dog's place? He would want the food that he was accustomed to, something warm to slip down his throat, and plenty of it, to have his aching feet rubbed, and all as quickly done as possible, that he might sleep and digest without interruption, and be on the march again three hours before daylight. Still imagining himself to be the slowest dog of the team, and resolved to do his best, Sandy drifted off to sleep.

Little Beaver seemed to be already aware of everything that the Corporal had advised Sandy. Perhaps it was intuition, perhaps a word from the far-sighted old Chief. Beaver was in favor of participating and of using a sixteen-dog hitch. In their ore-hauling business, in fairness to each of the four drivers, they had placed four dogs in each team that were the best specimens that the kennel possessed. These sixteen top-flight dogs should now be assembled in one super-hitch. Little Beaver had a deeper insight than Sandy into the natures and capabilities of dogs, and Sandy gave him a free hand in assigning the stations to the team. Also Beaver had a feeling for showmanship, the same inner urge that impels the Indian to paint himself in war color, and decorate himself with gaudy feathers and buckskin fringes.

It was a glorious collection of animals that the young Indian assembled. All were white, without blemish in coat, haunches, or forward-plumed tails; all children or grandchildren of Ne-Nu-Ka and the White Phantom. Beside the sixteen first-string animals Beaver chose four extras, to be substitutes should any first-stringers go lame or be injured during the trials or on the way to North Bay. The contrast between the nippy little leader, dancing effortlessly along on his slack line, looking hither and yon, observing the landscape like an idle tourist, without attempting to pull a pound of weight, and the bushy-shouldered phalanx behind him, was not only picturesque, but was an object lesson in the authority that brain exercises over muscle. Quicksilver was paid for what he knew, not for what he did.

Once the team had been chosen, Little Beaver took it out for a hard run each morning and afternoon, while Sandy took over other business. Between trips to the mine Oscar and Middle Beaver set to re-jointing and polishing the steel-runner komatik, and renewing the pads of the collars. They might win, or they might lose, but it would be a stunning equipage that drew up before the City Hall at North Bay.

The Captain telephoned Corporal Don the text of Mr. Brainard's rules, which cancelled one of Beaver's ideas, that they would include an alternate lead dog. As identically the same dogs must return to the finish line as had started, no substitutions along the way would be allowed. Another message from the Captain bothered the boys more than they liked to confess. Disquieting stories were current, he said, about a team entered by an Ojibway Indian, Limping Deer by name. Gamblers with money to spend were backing him to the limit. Three weeks before the event, it was reported that twenty thousand dollars had been bet on him to win. The real ugliness of the situation lay in the boasts of the Ojibway's friends, that any team good enough to be a serious rival would be violently put out of the running. While the Captain did not place too much confidence in these tales, his private advice to Beaver and Sandy was to bring their own dog food, to come armed, and to have trustworthy friends to guard their team night and day.

A day's ration for a hard-worked dog is from two to three pounds of fish, and a double handful of cooked corn meal. The Hudson's Bay Company used soft lead seals, the size and shape of a penny, with which to secure bales of furs during transport. Once the soft seal has been pressed over the ends of the fastenings, no one can tamper with the contents of a package, without it being noticed. Sandy packed his cured fish in sixty-pound sacks, sewed at each end with stout twine, and sealed with Company seals. Each package, therefore, represented one day's ration.

As it left Porcupine, the sled carried three men, their rifles, spare harness and tie chains, sleeping and cooking gear, and fish for twenty days. Sandy rode the runners, proud to be carrying no whip. He counted upon having ten free days to explore the itinerary, and to stage a full-dress rehearsal of the Race.

The nights between home and Cochrane they slept on the floors of friendly settlers' homes and stabled one day in the garage of the Intelligence Branch. The Captain did not say much, but the sunburned wrinkles around his eyes deepened, as he saw the make-up of the team, the extra guards they had brought along, and the care with which the partners had packaged their supplies. There was a restless night for the team in a baggage car, and again the hospitality of an army garage at North Bay.

The day of their arrival at North Bay, Sandy made one purchase. At a bookstore he bought a large-scale map of the districts of Dog Rib, Lac des Douze, Anvil, Brisket, Snidder's and Parker's Chapel. He meant to know the country roads and by-paths by heart. So long as the racers passed through the checking points of the circuit, which were at Dog Rib and Brisket, the Committee did not care what intermediate by-ways the drivers used.

That evening the boys lighted their candle at five o'clock. On the floor of the garage, with a piece of chalk, Sandy drew a plan of the country. Inclined toward him, almost touching the dim flame, were the faces of the two Indians and the half-breed. Not an inch of the chalkline but was photographed upon their memories.

"Tomorrow we try to get to Dog Rib," concluded Sandy. "From North Bay to Rufus there is but one road. We take that. But from Rufus to Stony Brook Bridge there seems to be three trails. We've got to decide which will be easier for a heavy team. The shortest route passes through a gorge which may be mushy and deep drifted. After Stony Bridge it is a straight pull on a travelled path into Dog Rib, where we will spend the following day, finding a family who will rent us lodgings for the first night of the race. I mean to leave Middle Beaver there, with corn meal and two sacks of fish, to be ready to feed when we arrive. At the stopovers during the race we shall probably rest about six hours, and we mustn't waste a second of it. While he feeds, I'll look after their feet. We'll tie them inside as a precaution, and he must sit up all night with a light. You other two, Oscar and Little Beaver, will do the same. From now on, we don't trust anyone, no matter how friendly he seems. Watch the fish and the meal like a lynx at a rabbit hole."

In the corner of the garage smouldered a fire, with a pan of beans and pork simmering upon it. A loaf of home-made bread stood near. Each of the four men took his claspknife from his pocket, stroked the blade upon his trouser leg, cut into the loaf of Mother Mackay's bread, and fed himself from the common dish with his knife, soaking up the liquid with sops of bread. Having eaten, they slept. Even in his sleep one of

Quicksilver's ears was cocked, as though he were afraid of missing something.

With the same care with which they had traced the best trail to Dog Rib, where they left Middle Beaver and his supplies with the MacTavish family, the three remaining members of the party proceeded over smooth ice to Anvil, where Oscar and his bundles were deposited among the excited little Callihans, who were delighted to be brought into contact with the nationally-famous contest. Climbing Adam's Apple was the hardest stretch the team had yet encountered. The heavy front-swing dogs repeatedly broke through the crust, and, although the sled was nearly empty, Sandy and Little Beaver ran the greater part of the distance.

At Brisket they found difficulty in locating lodgings. As there seemed no choice, they finally settled with a woman called Top-Knot Mary, who conducted a stopover house. She was surly, and demanded five dollars a night, in advance, for the use of her ground floor. A quarter-mile beyond was a cabin which appeared untenanted.

"Couldn't I rent that?" inquired Sandy.

"No, a man already has it, a man with dogs," answered the woman sourly.

"All right, here's your money, to bind the bargain," said Sandy. "For three nights. Tonight, that's one. I'll pass again in five days, that's two. Then I'll pass the third day of the race, if all goes well, and that's the third. My friend will stay here until the race is over, paying regular board."

The woman had a remark upon her tongue, but changed her mind. She was troubled over something.

Back in North Bay, Sandy rested the team for a day and a night, and then launched the full-dress rehearsal of the Work-Dog Race, as had been pre-arranged. His were heavy dogs, freighters, and not speed animals, but he was counting upon their endurance and prime condition, a light sled, the good and quick care they would receive at the halts, and their fresh familiarity with the route, to compensate for their weight. Such material as he had, he was trying to use intelligently. Quicksilver had his mother's gift for sticking to a trail that he had once travelled, and he would have been over the circuit twice in ten days.

The Race was announced to leave the City Hall at eight o'clock in the morning. Allowing for the usual social postponements, Sandy, on his dress rehearsal, quit that central building at eight-thirty, swinging out through the scattered frame houses at a smart trot. On the komatik were only the tie-chains, an emergency ration, and his sleeping bag. Traffic pulled aside to give him the right of way, men saluted, and women fluttered their handkerchiefs. The public had the Race very much on its mind. At Rufus, as had been decided, he took the middle trail to Stony Bridge, and drew up in front of the MacTavish door four hours after dark. Considering their late start, the dogs had done remarkably well. Quicksilver had not needed a single command as to direction. Somewhere between his ears, every twist of the road had been recorded.

After dogs and men had eaten, there were five minutes for a chat in the MacTavish main room, with the family peering breathlessly down through the cracks of the loft. At the end Middle Beaver crooked his finger and Sandy followed him outside. An Indian friend of Middle Beaver's, it seemed, had drifted into the clearing that afternoon. He told Beaver that he had been paid fifty dollars to conceal a deerhide into which hundreds of upright porcupine quills had been glued. He was to spread the skin at an elbow of the trail, and cover it lightly with loose snow, the instant that Sandy's team left the MacTavish door.

"He show ten bill. He do it, yes, but he tell me. By dead tree," explained Middle Beaver.

Had the animals trod upon the needles of that devilish contrivance the pads of their feet would have been punctured and the cuts would take months to heal. The Indian had said that the stranger was broad and tall, with a flattened nose and a blond beard. The money was new, ten five-dollar bills. Middle Beaver had counted them.

Sandy was scared. Who had paid this Indian to cripple their team? People with money and ruthless ways were fighting him.

"See your friend again," he ordered Middle Beaver, "and tell him to put the skin right opposite the big spruce stump. I know that turn, and I'll be on the lookout. But try to find who paid him."

All through the night, and the next day as he drove, the question tortured his mind. Who could have a grudge against him? And if this enemy were the sort of coward to vent his hatred upon harmless animals, where might he strike next? Ten new five-dollar bills! New bills? It stirred a recollection. And his chief rival was said to be an Ojibway.

The going to Anvil was rough, but Sandy at no time

pushed the team. A saying of the Old Racer had been: "To cover ground do not sprint. It is the steady trot and no stops that gets you there." At the Callihans', Oscar had seen or heard nothing to arouse suspicion.

The third day of the dress rehearsal was a punishing uphill scramble against the wind to Brisket. Sandy blew in after nine o'clock, but Little Beaver had everything warm and in order. Quicksilver had held the route like a magnet. While Little Beaver fed, and Sandy worked over the dogs' feet, the woman of the roadhouse stared with a hostile curiosity.

"All very fine, very fine here," Little Beaver announced loudly. "Top-Knot lady very fine, very fine."

For his partner, who never showed enthusiasm and who never spoke loud, to repeat this praise in almost a shout, was in itself astonishing. Sandy waited. Something was to be explained.

When they had stepped out of Mary's hearing the truth could be told. Little Beaver, during the previous night, had overheard someone talking to the woman behind the cabin. To his keen ears the words were distinct: "Just a few spoonfuls, sprinkled on the mush while it cooks. Here are the ten. You'll get as many more after the race." Through a crack in the floor he had later seen the woman, by the light of a candle, examine a packet of white powder, count a number of fresh green bills, and conceal both powder and money inside the wooden clock on the chimney piece. Beaver had stolen a sample of the drug and one of the bills, while Mary was getting firewood. She had not as yet noticed the theft. He did not know the source of the powder and the money but he had an idea that it was connected with the cabin up the road. Dogs had howled there during the night. Sandy took the sample and the stolen bill.

"Keep your eyes open, and sleep on your last sack of fish. When I come, on the race, I'll bring fresh meal from the North Bay store, and will use it at every stopover," were Sandy's last words.

The lap into North Bay was a deadly pull, although the road after Parker's Chapel was a much-travelled turnpike. Sandy let Quicksilver set his own pace. The boy himself was half-sick with fear and bitterness. It was the shots in the dark, the shots that he could not parry, that infuriated him. What was the use of wearing yourself out to make a fair race, if sneaks, with their tricks and poison, could steal it from honest dogs and drivers?

Once again in the city, as soon as he had groomed the team and locked the army garage, he insisted that the night man at the Intelligence Branch telephone the Lieutenant's home. Yes, he knew that it was after midnight, but this matter couldn't hold over until morning. After a walk and a delay, he confronted a sleepy officer in dressing gown and slippers. But the Lieutenant snapped wide awake when Sandy produced his evidence. The story of the porcupine quills, the white powder, the bill, left little doubt that the competing teams were to be threatened. Did this give substance to the rumored boasts of the gambling ring? Were those who might be winners against the Ojibway to be scared out or shot?

"It is now after one o'clock," meditated the officer. "The race is tomorrow at daylight. That doesn't give us much time. I will get word to the policeman at Noel's Gap, which is fifteen miles from Brisket, to cut across country and detain the man of the cabin as a suspect. But what ground have we for a detention?"

"Will you get Corporal Donaldson at Porcupine on the telephone right away?" requested the boy. "And read him the number on that bill. I have an idea."

The Intelligence Branch put through an official call.

At that hour of the morning the line was clear. Donaldson's dry tone answered almost at once.

"Corporal," began the Lieutenant, "I have beside me Sandy Mackay of your place. He has given me a new bill of five dollars. Numbered 487,529 BW. Have you anything to say about the series from which it comes?"

"A moment, Sir, until I get my notebook," the policeman replied. A short wait, then the Corporal again. Even over the telephone his auditors were startled by Donaldson's vehemence. "Yes, I have this to say; if you can lay hands upon the man who passed that money, you will have caught one of the worst scoundrels in Canada." The intelligence man listened, nodding his head, for another three minutes, and hung up.

"Don says that this bird is too quick on the trigger for a single man to bring in. We'll send three men from here in the morning. It will be slower, but they should have him in custody a full twenty-four hours before any of the racing teams strike Brisket."

Almost insensible with weariness, Sandy retraced his steps through the snowy streets. This was the morning before the great Race. The dogs were fed, thank Heaven. He would lock himself inside the garage and sleep until noon.

16. *Sandy Proves Himself*

THE SKY was overcast the next morning and people became apprehensive of a mid-winter thaw. But during the early hours of February sixteenth the weather turned clear and cold. The crust stiffened. Streams and lakes grew hard as crystal. The moon was nearing its full, and as much of the Race must be run before sunrise and after sunset, the light of the heavenly bodies would be of immense help.

The North Bay Winter Carnival was to run concurrently with the Race. The King and Queen of the Carnival would be upon their thrones to wave the dogs a farewell. Colored lights, snow statuary, the decorations of the Mayor's rostrum, and a military band made it a truly gala occasion. At eight o'clock late-comers were hurrying to their places along the curb or upon the official platform.

Many collections of dogs which had no expectation of winning were in City Hall Park. They had been entered out of compliment to the Committee, or to boost interest in their own particular breed, or as a gesture of patriotism. Any club or person who could muster ten adult animals, pose them long enough to be photographed and to trot a few blocks, was eligible. There were Newfoundlands, Pyrennean Shepherds, St. Bernards, Brie Shepherds, all shaggy, well-groomed creatures, but over-fed and not trained to sledging. In one of the teams the English Foxhound, with its famed staying power, was the dominant blood. In addition to the strictly working breeds, the Samoyedes, the Malemutes, the Eskimos, and the Siberian Huskies, were half-a-dozen crosses between the Workers and the larger Europeans, such as the Dane, the Mastiff, the Wolfhound, Boarhound and Staghound.

As Sandy ran his eye along the seventeen entries lined up before the judges' platform, picking out the teams that would be hard to beat, he discarded all but two. One was the Ojibway hitch which the spectacular betting had favored. The second was a nicely-graded, well-mannered cross between the Malemute and the Alsatian Shepherd. Save a miracle, the Race would be between these two teams and his own hitch of heavy-weights.

The boy sucked in his breath sharply, as he studied Limping Deer's outfit, dog by dog. Neither he, nor anyone present, had ever seen such grouped power and ferocity in a single team. Someone had been experimenting on breeds, yes, and for a long time. As near as Sandy could analyze their breeding, Limpy's animals were a cross between a half-bred timber wolf and Scotch Deerhounds. But to get them so uniform in type and color, they must be the selected best from many litters.

Caesar, the leader, weighed not less than a hundred and twenty pounds. The straightness of his forelegs, and the tan trimmings of his wire-haired, slate-grey coat, seemed a throw-back to the Dane. In him was less of the wolf, and more of the dog. That Limpy was afraid of him was obvious. He stood by the leader's head, tense to repel attack, whip in one hand, and the section of an axe handle in the other. Limpy wore double-thick, moosehide mittens, and Sandy would have wagered that his hands, inside, were bound with strips of deerskin. On either side of the team were four Indian helpers, also mittened and armed with clubs. Their duty was to insulate the dogs from spectators and other teams.

As to the speed and endurance of the Ojibway animals, Sandy could not judge, but he did not think that they would stand extreme cold. That they were professional fighters, stood out all over them. On a narrow piece of trail, any prudent driver would refuse to pass them. They were throat-grabbers—the brand of animal that, at a word from the driver, or perhaps without that word, would hurl themselves, as a single pair of jaws, upon a team that was outrunning them. That would be one way of deciding the race.

The second hitch that caught Sandy's fancy was a Malemute-Alsatian cross, bred and driven by a farmer from Fort Resolute, Felix Moore by name. They were docile, in fine condition, staunch on their legs, and, with no load, would be very fast. Whether they would have the stamina of his own team, Sandy questioned. But the driver was in a daze. As he stood by the veteran leader, Murdo, a dog that Sandy loved at first sight, Mr. Moore's eyes did not focus upon his surroundings. He was a sick man, quite sick, Sandy thought to himself.

Leaning against a nearby tree, her face showing deep anxiety, was Mrs. Moore. Sandy liked her, too. She was blue-eyed, with the shoulder droop that many farmer wives, mothers of big families, acquire in their thirties. After several timid starts, she came toward Sandy, and addressed him from behind his shoulder.

"You have a kind face, and I know that you will not leave him alone, out there. Promise me that you will get him back. He is too sick to go. But those dogs are his very life. He loves them more than the children and me. He borrowed the money to come. He feels that he must win, if it kills him. I have put a bottle of quinine in his knapsack. Promise that you will bring him back to us."

The bugle was sounding for the first team to start. Sandy nodded; he could say no more.

Early in the pageant, each driver had passed in procession before the Mayor's box, shaken hands with his Honor, with Mr. Brainard and the King of the Carnival, kissed the hand of the Queen and drawn a folded paper from the silver bowl she held. The numbers upon these slips determined the order of departure. At inter-

vals of three minutes the teams, one after the other,
would start. Limpy had drawn number three, Mr.
Moore number seven, Sandy number eight.

The lemon-tinted sun beamed. The air was crisply
transparent. The sprightly military march ended in a
fanfare. The crowd was friendly, and applauded every-
body and everything. It was a great show. For dog-
lovers it was a field-day. Soon the dogs would be gone,
and the audience could turn their cheerful thoughts to
marketing, school-teaching, offices and storekeeping,
forgetful of the two hundred dogs they had clapped
out upon the snow-bound bleakness. A few of the older
people were conscious of a deeper meaning, as they
saw their fellow-countrymen and the valiant beasts,
offering themselves for the nation's defense.

Starter Number One was the Pyrennean Shepherd
team. But as one of the ancient and honorable members, who had only been included to make up the number, sat down to scratch himself as the pistol cracked,
and refused to budge until the flea was found, the initial
send-off was not theatrical. Second to start was a collection of Irish and Scotch Deerhounds, driven by a
Welsh dentist of the city. Club members had been drill-
ing these champions during the past fortnight. The

crowd knew both dogs and driver, and gave them a warm send-off. They were not expected to go more than ten miles outside the city limits, but no one should intimate that the Irish, the Scotch, and the Welsh were not patriotic.

The start of the Ojibway team had been organized as a manifestation of tribe loyalty to the Government. Dignified chiefs, in full regalia, saluted the official stand. Sandy, standing twenty feet from Limpy, noticed several small, instructive details, as the Indian started his team. The sledge, save for two British flags, was absolutely naked: no food, no bedding, no spare harness. The driver, at convenient points along the route, would find everything he needed. The dogs were sullen, not used to strangers. Caesar, not Limpy, was the commander of the pack. Between driver and leader was always that solid bar of birchwood. But the breeding of those monster dogs, the planning of the patriotic show, the organization of the halts, all this, Sandy was positive, was not just the work of ordinary Ojibway Indians. In the background was a superior brain.

"Number Seven," announced the loud-speaker. The pistol rang out, and Murdo guided his light-footed mates in a beautiful curve between the lines of spectators. Mr. Moore, rigid as a statue, swayed on the rear runners, his face drawn and bony, like one of the picture-cards of St. Francis that the Pere Antoine gave to Porcupine children at christenings.

Sandy's turn, at last. Little black Quicksilver minced to the line, the white company at his heels. For style and for efficient appearance, no team approached them. Sandy had left his four substitutes and the extra food with the care-taker of the army garage. In a sort of dream he heard the announcer and the pistol, but most distinct was a voice from behind his shoulder, "God bless you. You won't leave him." The boy raised his arm. The Mayor returned the salute. But it wasn't meant for him. It was a foolish promise that Sandy was making to a family at Fort Resolute and to their mother.

Out through the suburbs, the amateur teams, in various embarrassments, were dropping out. As he slid along the smooth-packed roadway, that Quicksilver now knew by heart, Sandy was thinking of his team in relation to his two competitors. Each of the three drivers had a different problem. In his own case he knew that his team had endurance, they would plow along the trail as long as there was breath in their bodies.

But he did not know their speed. They had never been tried out with other dogs. His tactic would be to push steadily ahead, for long hours, at about their natural pace. They could not go much faster, but they never need go much slower. They might not win, but they would finish.

Mr. Moore's wisest plan, provided he were well enough to think at all, would be different. His dogs had speed, probably more speed than Limpy's or Sandy's. But he could not be sure that they had the second-and-third-wind that it takes to cover hundred-mile stages, day after day. His strategy would be to clamp upon the flank of another team, and trust to a fast sprint at the end.

As to Limping Deer, his was a special case. His dogs had power and willingness to fight, but Sandy surmised that their staying power and fleetness were unknown quantities, even to their driver. That Limpy had not handled them long was clear from his arm's-length manner with Caesar.

But from the porcupine quills of which Middle Beaver had learned, and from the poison that Little Beaver had discovered, Sandy was pretty sure that the owners, backers, and driver of the big team did not rely upon speed or endurance to win, in any honest way. They meant to conquer by tricks and crime. Assuming that there were other traps of the same nature as those of which he knew, Sandy was convinced that if he won it would be because of watchfulness, unhesitating self-defense, and good luck,—mostly good luck.

On the road to Rufus, the boy met but one trace of the Ojibway, who had a fifteen-minute start. Whenever he topped a hill, he looked far ahead, but nothing moving was in sight. Limpy must be following a secret route of his own, for at one spot the spoor of big feet cut obliquely across the main path. Mr. Moore, who was conserving the strength of his team, let Sandy pass him within an hour. Thereafter, Moore curled up on his sled and Quicksilver, with Murdo a hundred yards to the rear, set the pace, and showed the road throughout the day.

It was after ten o'clock when Sandy pulled up at a firelit doorway, where Middle Beaver, a lantern, and the smiling MacTavish family awaited him. Supper for dog and man had been ready to eat since five o'clock. They had seen nothing of Limping Deer. The final ten miles, Sandy had pushed Quicksilver a trifle, but Murdo was not to be shaken off. In the last rays of daylight he had seen Mr. Moore sitting up, giving orders. His fever seemed to be better. While Sandy wanted to be a good neighbor to the other white contestant, yet he did not forget that this was an important race, and that he was out to win. He had already done quite a lot for Mr. Moore, in guiding his team over the whole first lap.

Middle Beaver had news from his Indian friend. The stranger of the five-dollar bills had passed the day before, bringing a second quill-studded hide. He was upset, and wanted the place changed. Instead of at the angle by the stump, the skins were to be concealed, side-by-side, on a stretch of fair-running snow, where the drivers would be thinking of nothing but making speed. The new place was two miles beyond the stump, but there was no object to mark it. The Indian therefore proposed to stick two branches in the snow, fifty yards before the trap. On seeing the upright sticks the driver must dismount, and walk ahead until the quills were found.

But what of Mr. Moore, thought Sandy? He would have no warning of the deadfall. The boy therefore decided to start at three o'clock instead of four, to have his dogs checked at the forester's cabin, then hurry forward until the skins should be discovered and removed. That would clear the way for any racer who might come later.

It turned out that way, although the dogs grumbled at being re-harnessed after a five-hour rest. The committeemen were at their table, the lamp lighted. At the dead spruce corner Sandy slowed down. A mile and a half farther, he dismounted, put his hand on Quicksilver's head, and stepped cautiously forward, scuffing his feet. The shadows were too thick to distinguish the branches, but suddenly a spine, sharp as steel, pierced his mukluk. He brushed aside the snow and found the two hides, frozen like boards. It would not have been possible for a team to pass uninjured.

As he was bending the skins into a bundle, his dogs raised their muzzles in the howl-salute to an approaching team. Murdo and his mates came flying by. They certainly had speed. The man did not seem to see Sandy, nor anything else, for that matter. His face, bony and expressionless as a corpse, was fixed upon the path ahead. He looked very sick, but he had managed to make an early start.

During the second day of the Race, over the ice of the Lac des Douze into Anvil, Sandy caught no sight of either competitor. This was ideal going for a speedy team. The boy was discouraged, for he felt that he was being outrun by Mr. Moore's dogs, and being outwitted by Limpy's knowledge of the short-cuts. He rested the team twice, himself chewing a frozen sausage and a cracker. At Anvil, Oscar had fish and mush ready to ladle out upon clean planks. Everyone around the Callihan cabin was so sincere and above-board that he had not the heart to insist upon their cooking the fresh supply of meal that he had brought. They had seen no other teams, but neighbors had seen stranger Indians, with rifles, wandering in the woods. Being a target for sharpshooters was what worried Sandy the most. The fact that no one had so far taken a pot shot at him was discouraging proof that he was behind the Ojibways, as he was also behind the Alsatians.

He had rather expected to overtake Mr. Moore on the climb over Adam's Apple, and he did. This was the sort of going that took downright stamina, such as his dogs had. Gallant old Murdo, badly winded, his claws split, could not keep his footing on the steep and glistening crust. The driver sat motionless upon the sled, not more than half-awake. Sandy shouted a hail, but he did not turn his head. Murdo sang his pleasure in having company and a pacemaker, and swung into Quicksilver's footsteps.

At Brisket, Top-Knot Mary was stamping with rage. She refused to let the dogs in. Policemen had been at her house that afternoon, and there was nothing she detested more than attention from the police. More than that, they had induced her to show them Limpy's hide-out for the night. She was in terror of her life. The officers had gone to wait for Limpy, and the bearded man of the cabin, who was Limpy's boss, would strangle her with as little thought as he would eat an apple.

The police had said nothing, but something serious must have happened. With bad men about, policemen got shot, which was healthy for no one. Even during the woman's tantrum, Little Beaver had not left the dog ration he was dishing out. He could vouch for it. Sometime during the preceding night, he said, a sergeant and three men, guided by a colonist, had come to the other cabin. They were terribly keen on catching up with Limpy Deer.

Little Beaver had the dogs snapped to the extension line, and the bottle filled with coffee, when he woke Sandy at half-past three. The Indian had been awake all night, guarding the team. In the other cabin there had been a light, and he thought there was a sentinel. Sandy was a silent and thoughtful boy at the Brisket forester's office when he checked through.

It was too far, and the light too poor to see clearly, but Sandy fancied that the skeleton shape of a komatik was outlined in front of the other house as he galloped by. An armed figure stood outside.

It was the fourth and final day. He and Ne-Nu-Ka's children would be victors, or mere also-rans, before they slept again. To the best of his knowledge he was the hindermost of the three teams. One could not wish for finer weather. He was nearly to Snidder's when one dog after another raised his snout and howled. They had smelled, before he had seen, the abandoned sledge beside the trail. In front of it were the mounds that indicated a team asleep in harness. A larger mound, blanketed by snow dust, lay on the lee side of the sled. It was Mr. Moore's outfit. They had spent the night out, digging in where Murdo had halted. The dogs were shaking themselves and stretching, but the larger bundle which was the man did not stir. Sandy's first act was to run ahead, pulling off his mitten, to feel inside the sleeping bag, and touch the skin of the man's face and neck. It was burning hot. Mr. Moore was alive, but in a high fever. His lips moved, but said nothing.

Sandy's brain was clicking. He had a race to win. And it had to be won in the next few hours. Others were counting upon him. The Ojibway was ahead. But here was a man in delirium. A promise was a promise. As he was thinking he automatically ripped the end from the sack containing his emergency ration, and tossed chunks of fish to Murdo and the others.

Pulling the man to a sitting position against the sled, he poured hot coffee down his throat. From the knapsack he retrieved the bottle of quinine. He didn't know whether it was good medicine or bad, nor how much to give. But he put four capsules in Mr. Moore's mouth, washing it down with more of the black coffee. He brought his own sled alongside, lashed on the man's body, still in its sleeping bag, pillowing the head upon the roll of deerhide. They were ready.

Quicksilver obeyed the whistle, and moved ahead. Murdo fell into his station behind. Revived by the mouthful of breakfast, by the lightened sled, and above all, by the companionship of another team, the Moore dogs showed themselves able to match any pace that Quicksilver might be able to set.

At two o'clock, while the dogs took a breather, Sandy gave the sick man more of the hot drink, and more quinine. He himself munched a sausage and a cracker, while he took stock of the situation. The fact that he had not been molested, nor shot at, convinced

Sandy that he was no longer a dangerous rival of Limpy. They weren't bothering about him; he was too far behind.

An hour after Parker's Chapel he would have to pass an exposed spot, the only dangerous one left. Here a ravine along the course of a brook offered cover for

sharpshooters. If by any chance he were ahead, this was the last opportunity for the Indians to get him. He believed that he was behind, but he could not be sure, and his heart throbbed in his throat as Quicksilver swerved into the bottleneck of the gorge.

Crack! A hatful of smoke hung above a cluster of rock, a hundred yards from the trail. Quicksilver, a black ball, was rolling end over end. For a split instant the upper half of a leering face was visible, then a shadow dodging among the tree trunks. The rifleman had done his job; he had crippled the lead dog of the team that was heading Limpy in. To Sandy, untying Quicksilver and laying him beside Mr. Moore, it was sickening. But the Indian had aimed high. The bullet had plowed a furrow across the dog's back, and he was bleeding profusely, but the bone was no more than nicked. As the boy's fingers told him these reassuring details, he realized that the attack meant that he was ahead! They had to stop him! But they shouldn't.

Here was a new question. Should he put Murdo in Quicksilver's place? No, it was his team, his race. Moreover, each team, driver and dogs together, said the rules, must compete as a unit, without outside help.

He was well past Parker's Chapel, no more than twenty-five miles from North Bay. That was the same distance as Porcupine from the Three Brothers Mine. He himself could run that. Winding the end of Quicksilver's free line around his mitten, he stepped out in front. He would lead his own team in.

Nine miles from North Bay, at the terminus of the telephone line, lived a storekeeper. With this merchant Mr. Brainard had arranged that when the first incoming team should pass his shop he should call up the committee. Sufficient time would thus be given for illuminating the park and the avenue, for the band to warm up their instruments, for dignitaries to arrive, and for the King and Queen of the Carnival to don their tinsel finery.

Cheers rippled along the curbstones, marking the team's progress. Onlookers stared. This was no dashing finale of a Race. First ran a boy, nosed forward by a line of white dogs. On his sledge lay the bundled form of a man, and a cock-eared black dog. Behind, trotted a driverless team. The square was brilliant with the reflection of colored bulbs upon ice-laden trees and snow statuary, upon the gold braid of the military and the instruments of the band. But the heavy-footed boy did not look up. He was trying to decide a hard question.

Thirty feet from the finish line he slowed down and did an odd thing. Saluting the officials, he lifted the black dog from his sledge and tied him in as leader of the white team. The dog wobbled on his hind quarters, but could stand. Next, the boy led Murdo and the second hitch alongside his own sledge and, with the help of a woman who ran out from the crowd, transferred the man in the sleeping bag to Murdo's sledge.

This kid, whoever he might be, was staging a great act. As Sandy spoke, the silence was absolute.

"Mr. Moore and his team will cross the line first. No

one but Murdo and Mr. Moore have conducted his team around the circuit. Announce it," he said to the man at the loud-speaker.

Under his breath, Sandy clucked to Murdo, who walked sedately forward. The woman was crying.

"We want this Race to be a tie," continued Sandy evenly. "Will the timekeepers please give me the signal, so that Quicksilver can cross the line exactly three minutes after Murdo. We started three minutes behind him, and we want to finish the same way."

People nudged one another and leaned forward. They had hoped for a thrill, but this was prodigious.

Quicksilver trotted unsteadily under the tape. The announcer threw away his typewritten program, and shouted, "Three cheers for Murdo Moore and Quicksilver Mackay. Let's go! Hip, Hip . . . ." To Sandy, as he lifted the black dog back upon the sled, it made sweeter music than the band. Mrs. Moore, hurrying her husband to the hospital, waved from the taxi window. He had kept his promise.

But where was the Ojibway team? The question was on everyone's lips. The chiefs, who had been assured that Limpy could not lose, stood on the sidelines like bewildered children. In their war bonnets they were awkwardly out of place without a winner. They were honest old men, but it would be four days before they learned the sensational truth. The gamblers who had placed the thousand-dollar bets strode up and down, gnawing their fingernails.

"Hello, Sandy. Congratulations!" The Captain and the Lieutenant fell into step with the boy as he turned his team into the army garage. "Look behind you. You've still got old Murdo and his lot trailing you."

"We don't get the point," added the Lieutenant. "Why on earth did you make it a dead heat?"

"I didn't want any difference between the teams," said Sandy. "When it comes to giving out the contracts, you know. You and the Clubs will need six teams to get the scout patrol going. Mr. Moore must have at least two. We have four. There aren't any others in the same class. With the Race a tie, it can all be closed up in ten minutes."

"Smart boy!" exclaimed the officers. "Come in and talk it over with the Club secretaries and us in the morning. Mrs. Moore can act for her husband. Why don't you try a good night's sleep for a change?"

"I won't need to try," grinned Sandy, as he started to feed both teams.

17. Death in the Cabin

THREE days later Sergeant Bradford returned to North Bay and made his report to his superiors of the Intelligence Branch. The Sergeant was accompanied by Little Beaver, who, with Sandy, was present as a witness when the oral report was delivered.

Bradford reconstructed the events preceding the death of the bearded man, from circumstantial evidence collected by himself on his arrival at the cabin. Information as to the origin of the so-called Ojibway Dog Team, and of the conspiracy to win the Work-Dog Race, was furnished by Limping Deer, detained by the police as a material witness and member of the conspiracy. This information was subsequently confirmed by the police at the Athabaskan farm of the Ossian Brothers.

Sergeant Bradford and two men left North Bay for Brisket the day before the start of the Race. As far as Snidder's they were able to travel by caterpillar tractor. The policeman from Noel's Gap, and a farmer acquainted with the country, joined them before the end of the journey. They were five men, well armed. They knocked at the cabin about two o'clock in the morning of the day before any racer could pass Brisket. Inside it was dark, but desultory smoke drifted from the chimney. There was no reply to their order to unbar the door. Quick, swishing movements, however, could be heard within.

With an axe the colonist hewed an entrance. The interior, as the flashlights revealed it, resembled a slaughter-house. The scent of meat and blood was warm and heavy. Embers of an expiring fire gave some light. Upon the table was an empty bottle and a glass. Under the table was a second bottle, splintered but still holding the dregs of liquor, and the twisted body of a man, arms and legs spread-eagled. His bearded head and right forearm were practically severed. Behind him, suspended from a rafter, was the carcass of a young doe.

Eight glaring eyes, bunched in the corner, within a three-foot circle, were the sole signs of life. The torches showed a confused mass of wire-haired legs and ribs, white teeth and red tongues. Four gigantic animals had been starved to two-thirds their natural weight. As the men edged cautiously into the room, leaving behind them a lane of moonlight to the open door, the four beasts, with a unity of movement that spoke of pack hunting, launched themselves toward the opening. To them that unguarded door meant freedom, the open forest, a new birth into life. The men of the law leaped aside as the animals dashed through the door.

As the Sergeant reconstructed the events leading up to Butch's death, it seemed clear that the blond giant had been starving the four wolf-dogs in preparation for loosing them on the team of any dangerous rival. The carcass of the doe, hanging out of their reach, had been intended to incite them further. Butch had been drinking heavily, and whether he had freed the dogs himself in a fit of drunken madness, or whether he had fallen asleep and they had been able to slip their emaciated heads through their collars, would never be known.

The history of the Ojibway dogs was simple when

explained. Years before, in Athabaska, Butch had made the acquaintance of the eccentric Ossian Brothers. Their hobby, as rough-and-ready scientists, was the crossing of wolf blood with females of heavy European breeds. They owned, in captivity, fine specimens of the polar and the timber wolf. The object of the experimenters, on their remote farm, was to determine how large a percentage of wolf blood might be added to a domestic breed, and still have the offspring safe, and useful for man's work. They desired their pups to be as resistant to inclement weather and as economical to feed as were the wild animals, and yet to fall within the classification of dogs. Sometimes, of course, the experimenters went too far. The pups would be over the line, more wolf than dog, and too vicious for man to handle. But they did develop many hardy and powerful specimens.

Butch, upon learning of the Work-Dog Race, and upon conceiving his campaign to win it, got in touch with the Ossians. He wanted a team that would be stunning to the eye, to stimulate the gamblers. The brothers had such a team. Whether the animals were fast and capable of long hauls, was secondary, for Butch meant to insure victory by outside means.

★ ★ ★

A recent letter from Bumbly Bill's Sally, up in Porcupine, says that Sergeant Sandy Mackay is now responsible for the operation of the Atlantic Division of the patrols. He varies the routes each week, farther north or farther south, to keep an eye upon the widest possible expanse of territory. Corporal Little Beaver is in charge of the breeding kennels, where new dogs are recruited for all three Divisions. Felix Moore is with his houseful of children at Fort Resolute, but every few months he sends Little Beaver a couple of fine Malemute-Alsatians for training. Murdo II is one of the brainiest lead dogs of the service. Among the drivers are Oscar, Middle Beaver, and Sally's brother, Antoine, named after the good priest who baptized him. The half-team which Sergeant Mackay uses on his inspection trips is captained by Quicksilver Mackay, the dog in a hundred thousand.